FINAL DAYS

FREEZE

ELLIS KROSS

E / K

. . .

First Edition, October 2014
Written by Ellis Kross
Edited by Sidonie Lailler

PUBLISHED BY ELLIS/KROSS

ISBN: 978-0-9905356-2-1
Kross, Ellis, 1983—
Freeze: Final Days
I. Title. Fiction. Science-Fiction/Thriller

ISBN: 978-0-9905356-2-1 pbk.

Story by Ellis Kross
Book Design by Izzy
Interior Photograph by Collage_Best (istockphoto.com)
Cover Photography by suteishi (istockphoto.com)

Written at the Crow's Nest.

Printed in the United States
10 9 8 7 6 **5** 4 3 2 1

. . .

Final Days

Freeze Volume 2

CHLOE wondered if this was what it felt like for her father when they reunited after fifteen years of estrangement.

Although it hadn't been fifteen years for her—in fact, it had only been two years apart from Aaron—it sure as hell felt like fifteen years. . . even more.

The monotony of the past two years spent in Death Valley certainly had a way of drawing out time as if time itself was a grain of sand falling through an hourglass. Days consisted of routine, an onerous pattern that Chloe had learned to kick in a former life. But it was back in her life—*this* life—more routine.

The last time Chloe saw her son was when he was sixteen; and, at the time, he was about as close to his mother as any bestie. Time had drawn out since then. Structures had fortified. Powers privatized. New policies came and went, most of them regulated by the filthy hands of corruption. The rich got richer. The poor got poorer. Compromise had become a garden-variety mask to disguise the truth, and a once shrugable term like *under the table* had become a staple in the way of law.

After the assassination of President Robert Shaw on the nineteenth of March 2015, it was fair to say that things had changed for the worse, not the better.

Most importantly, her son had changed.

And so had Chloe.

When she first saw Aaron and Aaron first saw his mother, they could hardly recognize one another. Aaron couldn't believe how much his mother had deteriorated over the span of two years. Her hair had more gray in it. Her skin had very little color, almost pale. She had two small dots on the corners below each lower eyelid from where they had punctured her with needles. Every wrinkle told a story of tragedy, pain, and sadness. They fingered outward in wayward fashion, each wrinkle running like a creek along the corners of her face. The deeper the wrinkle ran, the deeper the story cut.

And Chloe had many cuts, but none that could be seen on the outside.

On the other hand, Chloe couldn't believe how much her son had grown—at least four inches, maybe five. The boyish face that she once knew and loved and dreamed about during sleepless nights in her cell was now stretched out in immaculate formation. The face was *not* the face Chloe had remembered. It was strange to her, new. His voice was much different too—resonant like his father's, no cracks, just a little wear and tear.

Amazing how two years could change a boy into a man.

But time had drawn out since then and it certainly hadn't been so forgiving to Chloe, as she would suspect . . .

RECAP/ROADS

IF you, Reader, have gotten this far into the story of Freeze, perhaps you're willing to delve a little farther. However, you must remember that time is of the essence. So, I assure you, Reader, I will abridge as best I can, for the fate of the human race hangs in the balance; and you alone, Reader, hold the key to our very existence. In addition, fearless Reader, continuing to proceed forward from this point is a choice of your own doing. So, remember: you will always have a choice; and it is choice that separates *us* from *them*. If you are not one of them, there is *still* a chance. The choice is yours, Reader, and yours alone.

Would you like to proceed? *Yes* or *No.*

Y

The last you read about our darling in distress, Diana Hailey Roth, who's name was later changed to Anne Roth, was that she finally, after fifteen years of estrangement, made amends with her ailing father, Leon Dorsey, who— you've previously learned over a series of exclusive interviews conducted by Renny Jacobson, a young pessimistic journalist from the magazine, *Flashback*—was once

known as the legendary crime fighter, Freeze. These interviews were deliberately recorded not for *Flashback*, but
for his daughter—now twenty-four—to help her remember
her childhood after she ran away from Whisperfront,
Maine. The events proceeding after she left Whisperfront
were dire, to say the least. Anne was involved in a horrific
car accident, which left her with severe amnesia—
ultimately turning her into an orphan. What her father
failed to acknowledge was that he had a spider creeping
over his shoulder, and it would do anything in its power to
obtain a rare artifact that he held in his possession. The
interviews were later captured on a USB flash drive, the
same one Anne later discovered on a hired gun who broke
into her house in the middle of the night and tried to murder her. Little did the hired gun know what he was up
against... That hired gun was working for a mysterious
individual called the Voice, a man with many names and
many faces. Later, we discovered that the Voice was actually the head steward of Leon's residence, Leatherby
Manor, as well as Leon's longtime confidant. His name
was Diego Tovar, but he was also known as the jungle
spider for his uncanny ability to sneak up on his prey and
kill them where they stood; he was a confidence man with
strong ties to one of South America's deadliest cartels; and
it was he, Diego, who revealed to his longtime confidant
that he was working in cahoots with JeneCorp, a ruthless
organization simply known as the Company. It was also
he, Diego, *not* Leon's former mentor and friend, Marcus
Hopkins, who informed JeneCorp about Leon's whereabouts after an early retirement from the spotlight, which
inevitably resulted in the deaths of Leon's wife, Isabel,
and his son, Dominic, as well as his own ultimate demise
many years later. We also learned that Diego had other
motives besides helping Leon fulfill his last dying wish of
rekindling with his daughter—those motives: to seek a
lifelong revenge against the United States of America; but
you, Reader, now know them as the *Dead Zones*, the place
that we do not talk about.

Before Leon's untimely death, Anne rekindled with her father whom she hadn't seen in fifteen years. Anne listened to the contents on the USB flash drive, the interviews; and they worked, as planned. Anne remembered her past through the stories her father had spoken of during the interview with Renny Jacobson. However, there was darkness in her past, crueler than any other darkness, one that Anne wished she had *not* remembered. Needless to say, we will get to that shortly.

Anne, now wanted for questioning by the authorities, buried her father's body where no one could find him and then escaped from police in the nick of time.

If you have gotten this far, Reader, all of this is mere refreshment.

Let it be told, though.

Anne's journey *never* stopped in Maine.

Her journey had just begun!

So, now that you know a little more about Anne and her history, we will continue the story four months later in Anodes, a small town forty miles south of Flagstaff where Anne sought refuge from the law.

For a little while, things seemed peachy for Anne. She found a suitable job as a part-time waitress at Phil and Tony's Bar and Grill. Phil's older sister, Miranda, hooked up Anne with a two-bedroom apartment—all furnished, of course. It wasn't much of a place; in fact, it was a dump. It had a roof that leaked whenever the tenant directly above her flushed the toilet or ran a faucet. It had a fairly decent size bathroom, but it was mostly covered in mold. And it had a faint stench of ammonia lingering in the air, as if something fat had died behind the walls. Half of the time the water heater didn't work, and Anne had gotten used to taking cold showers. In the loft directly above her lived a heel walker. It wasn't the most ideal place to live for anybody, especially a young woman; but for Anne, it was not only a roof over her head, but also a place to sleep. It took her twenty-four years to realize that materials were materials and that materials never brought her happiness. So, I guess it was fair to say that what happened in Lansford changed her for the better. She ended up dying her hair brunette and rescuing a two-year-old black Labrador. She named the dog Harley Jr.—who'd later be known as Pegasus after her soon-to-be discovery. Anne even changed her name from Anne Roth to her birth name, Jaelene Chloe Dorsey, after she buried her father in Maine. So, Chloe, *not* Anne, like many people in Anodes, was "getting by." And for Chloe, that was all that mattered, getting by without a fuss. And getting by was what Chloe did, but only for a little while. About a month after she settled in Anodes, Chloe thought the worst was behind her. She had made peace with the death of her estranged father; but, as before in Lansford, there was something missing in her life. Not once did she go through an entire day without thinking about her past, about that car accident after she ran away from Whisperfront or trying to fill in the blanks (amnesia had a funny way of filling in the *wrong* blanks) about Louis Bringer and what he had done to her many years ago after she left the orphanage, and, most importantly, about Sam, the strange boy whom she met at the hospital. Her father told her, "Move on," and that was exactly what she did—or at least tried to do. However, like the creeping three o'clock feeling that tormented her during the many hours spent at her previous job, USR, Louis would occasionally poke his head and force her to remember her dark past and the awful things he had done to her. Chloe didn't feel it as strongly as before—*that feeling*. It was there, though, creeping through her nerves at random hours of the day. If it was from a customer's remark or the way someone dressed or the way he or she acted or anything that reminded Chloe of Louis, she was still haunted by this man, this creature teetering throughout the lost hallways of her mind.

These manifestations were professionally known as "triggers," and they would forever live inside Chloe.

But Chloe would soon learn that history had a particular way of repeating itself.

On the thirteenth of February, 2015—a Friday—things took a turn for the worse. What better luck! On Friday the 13th, *they* found her. And if they could find her, then *he* could find her.

Chloe was on the way back to her apartment when she came across the February issue of *Flashback* on the newsstand outside a bookstore, USED READS. On the cover was an older photograph of her father, which was taken in his prime as Freeze: a debonair man dressed in a glimmering silver suit, hair gelled over his glossy scalp, eyes like sapphires.

The caption below: "A WEEK WITH MR. HOPKINS."

Chloe skimmed through Renny Jacobson's article, which consisted of the same interviews they shared in Leatherby Manor. Even her birth name, as well as her foster name, Anne Roth, as well as her troubling background, was mentioned in the article. Chloe assumed that she was fine. The townspeople of Anodes would never put the two together. There were a lot of Chloe's out there. Right? So, it was no big deal. Soon, the story would pass as most stories do. Right? Chloe wished she was right, but she was dead wrong. And that was when they came for Chloe, the Company. But first let's talk about how Chloe ended up in Anodes to begin with. . .

—

THAT morning after Chloe paid a visit to the Main National Bank in Lancaster, a town outside Sanford, Maine, and retrieved the CD along with a piece of paper with a certain address, Chloe drove south along the rambling East Coast until she found shelter in Springfield, Massachusetts. She decided to keep her head down for two days—mostly living off scraps and loose change. This, of course, was not new to her—in fact, as a young girl living on the run, she had grown accustomed to living like a vagabond. It almost came, shall I say, natural. She spent most of her days surviving off junk food and most of her nights listening to the CD that her father had made for her. In those days, Chloe learned certain tips and procedures on how to properly use the gaze to her advantage—

the "*ABCs.*" And if she learned how to master the gaze, then a commodity such as food or water or even money could be easily obtained.

Like stealing candy from a baby, it wasn't really stealing if the baby couldn't remember.

———

EXCEPT for Diego or any others Chloe had mistakenly used the gaze on, the first time she consciously used the gaze on a person was in New Haven, Connecticut, when she ran out of gas, as well as money. Chloe needed a little dough to get by, but not enough to draw any suspicion. So, late one night, she found a scrappy-looking clerk and used the gaze on him. The clerk told Chloe to take as much as she wanted—"It's yours," he said—as well as all of the money in the register, which was around three hundred dollars and some change. *It's all yours.* After she gazed the frightened man, something terrible happened to him. . . It started with a nosebleed. . . a single drop of blood slowly trickling from the clerk's nose and then more blood gradually streaming from his nose, as if she broke a levee inside his nose. It reminded her of that one guy—the hillbilly whom she had roughed up at a gas station outside Whisperfront—but the only difference between the two was that the clerk's nosebleed was *not* brought on by blunt force trauma. He was hemorrhaging from severe pressure. Next thing Chloe knew, he was convulsing on the floor and foaming from the mouth. Eventually, the clerk lost consciousness.

She didn't kill him, though.

Chloe made sure of it.

Yet, she forced the poor man into a state of shock.

When she checked on his condition, she saw the band on his ring finger.

He probably had a kid too, she thought, *maybe a whole litter of them.*

What other reason would he be working the graveyard shift?

This was all new to her as well, the thinking part.

Once Chloe learned how to use the gaze, her thoughts were much different, more vivid and clear, as if they were playing in real-time. She was—more or less—a spectator standing outside her body, watching and waiting.

She was so freaked out from what she had done to the clerk that she left the money behind and split before the cops arrived.

From there, she kept driving south.

—

IN Yonkers, New York, Chloe found another Sable like hers and changed the tags on the rental car as well. She assumed the cops were looking for her, especially after what went down in Whisperfront, and, of course, what happened in Lansford—the murders and whatnot. She didn't bother stopping in the Big Apple, although she had dreamed about traveling to the city when she was just a teenager.

Right now, the only thing on Chloe's mind was surviving, *not* sightseeing.

So, she kept moving.

And moving meant living. . .

—

BY the time Chloe reached Rockville, Maryland, she came down with a debilitating fever.

Chloe wanted to rest, but she had to keep moving.

She ended up driving through the night until the sun broke free from the horizon.

—

THE following day, she was crippled by a nasty stomach bug in Richmond, Virginia.

The bug lasted precisely twenty-four hours.

On the CD, her father specifically told her that it was one of the many side effects of the gaze.

He said that it was her body's way of adjusting to the gaze—this "new sense," as he called it.

—

AFTER she barely made it out of the state of Virginia, she traveled through the Tar Heel state, North Carolina, without stopping and then found a resting place in Columbia, South Carolina.

There, in Columbia, Chloe again stayed off the radar for a couple of weeks—hardly showing her face during the day and mostly coming out at night.

—

AFTER her time spent in the Palmetto State, she kept moving south. She spent the holidays by herself, except for Christmas. Thanksgiving was—by far—the loneliest day Chloe had spent on the road. Some people hugged it out. Some people cried it out. Some people yelled it out. Some people *ate* it out. These were all useful methods on how one could relieve the burden of loneliness. Then, there were others, like Chloe Dorsey, who did none of those things. All she did was listen. She listened to the sound of her father's voice, which brought her comfort and made her feel, if only a tad bit, *less* lonely.

—

THE morning after Thanksgiving in Macon, Georgia, she found a local Cantonese restaurant whose owners had tossed out an entire duck. The thing was seasoned to near perfection. Chloe hadn't eaten so well in months. It wasn't a turkey, as she had hoped for, but it was damn near close enough. And for that, Chloe *was* thankful— damn thankful. That morning was spent chowing down on duck legs in the back of a desolate parking garage and

listening to the voice of her father—even though she had
already listened to the CD in its entirety at least six or
seven times. Of all the days spent on the lonely road, the
day after Thanksgiving was the most rewarding. She had
food and a roof over her head—although a car roof, it was
a roof nonetheless—and the spirit of her father to keep her
company. For Chloe, if it wasn't for the simple things in
life such as food or shelter, more than likely Chloe
wouldn't have survived. She focused most of her listening
to the latter part of the CD, around the fifty-eight-minute
mark where her father started talking about these "others," the ones he had uttered right before he passed away.
There were five others, Chloe learned, all scattered
around the globe, one in France. In the back of her mind,
Chloe wasn't surprised. Not at all. Leon was a handsome
man. He was young and famous, and surely he was with a
lot of women before her mother. It happens. . .

—

CHLOE left the Peach State and stayed off the radar until
she reached Louisiana.

It was fair to say that Chloe liked the Bayou State,
liked its mystical and yet deathly charm. She liked its
grit as well. She liked the people too, except for maybe
one or two rotten souls; but you'll hear about those devils
shortly.

For about a month—twenty-seven days to be exact—
Chloe stayed in Sinclair Leprieur, a spit of a town a few
miles outside Baton Rouge, where she befriended a behe-
moth named Mighty Tiny, or just *Tiny* (don't let the name
fool you. Tiny was *not* so tiny. Nobody really knew his
name. Fact: Nobody had the cojones to ask, except for
Chloe, who promised Tiny never to tell anybody his name.
The name was their own little secret. Tiny was roughly
six feet six inches, shaped like a fridge, with a heart like a
prizefighter). Chloe spent Christmas in Sinclair Leprieur
with Tiny and his *not* so tiny family (the meal Tiny's
mother had cooked consisted of a typical Creole dinner: a

hearty gumbo with oyster dressing and corn pudding and enough food to feed a fucking army, and don't forget, the bûche de Noël for dessert). Mighty Tiny's line of work never restricted him from indulging from time to time; in fact, the boss encouraged it. He worked as a bouncer at a hole-in-the-wall exotic nightclub called the Flaming Eagle. He and Chloe met one night when she was dumpster diving just outside the nightspot. Her father would be ashamed, Chloe knew; but Chloe had *another* agenda on her mind, one she had come up with from spending her days on the road. When Tiny saw Chloe's state, her disheveled appearance—her raggedy clothes and whatnot— he saw an attractive woman underneath all of that dirt and grime. He introduced Chloe to his good pal, Nile Bundle, owner of the Flaming Eagle. Nile rallied a couple of his female friends; and they cleaned Chloe up good— "dolled" her up, if you will—and then he offered her a job at the Flaming Eagle. Even though Chloe was trying to keep a low profile, she took the job, a dancing gig, however, with a slight catch. She was convinced that she would be taken care of—"treated like *royal*ty," he told her. She was also told if any customers were to touch her inappropriately, then her friend, Tiny, would be in close proximity to put them in their place. But what these customers didn't exactly realize was that Tiny was the *least* of their worries. She was skeptical about taking the job at first. Tiny told her it was just tits and ass. Chloe wasn't the least bothered by them. She wasn't as large as the other girls, but they were big enough to shake and bounce and jiggle. It was fair to say that Chloe received enjoyment out of dancing. After all, it was one of the few perks the nightlife had to offer a twenty-something; and Chloe got paid too, even though it was done topless in front of horny fishermen who were mostly, if not, all married. She assumed either they didn't get enough action at home from the wife or—on the contrary—the wife couldn't get *it* up for them. So, they resorted to coming here and then taking *it* back home to the wife as if *it* was an anniversary gift. Wrap *it* up in a box, stick a cute little red bow on *it*, and do what you will with *it*.

Spending weeks alone on the road not only gave her time to practice the gaze on other life forms such as stray alley cats or rats or even cockroaches—any living thing with eyes—but it also gave Chloe time to control the gaze, as her father had taught her. . .

A strange illness plagued Sinclair Leprieur days after Chloe landed her new dancing gig at the Flaming Eagle. Two factors were involved—one, all of the patients who were showing up at the doctor's office were males from ages eighteen to fifty; and two, their symptoms were all the same—their dicks were as hard as batons. . . literally. For the ones who didn't receive the gaze during a state of arousal, the thing hung there on the side of their leg like a bloated sausage. When the doc asked if they had taken any male enhancement drugs such as the blue pill, their answers were the same as the next. What the hell could cause a man to have an everlasting boner? The answer: you got it—Chloe, or best known as the young and lovely, "Ms. Snake Eyes." Chloe's theme music: "*Far From Any Road*," sung by the band, the Handsome Family. The doctor, of course, was as perturbed as the nurses. In all the years of practice, he and his staff had never seen anything like it. The skin along the erected shaft was too hard to be pierced by a needle. From there, Reader, I will leave it up to you to figure out the only remedy the doctor had in mind. Eventually, the word had circulated around Sinclair Leprieur about the Flaming Eagle. Surprisingly enough, the nightspot still got business. Tripled its regular clientele. And that wasn't when Chloe skipped town, when she was getting too much attention, even though it seemed properly to do so. She left because of what happened that one night when she was taking a smoke break after her performance. She was minding her own business when all of a sudden two strange men approached her from behind. *Little* did they know who she was and what she was capable of doing to a man. Her emotions got the best of her that night and she accidentally gazed one of the men.

If she ranked the gaze from 1-10, 10 being the most powerful, she was cranked up to about a 7 or 8. She turned the man's two legs into stone, both of them attached to the asphalt as if they had been paved with the parking lot. If that wasn't enough to whet Chloe's sweet revenge. . .

His name was Jason Swight.

The locals called him Jay Bird because he had a wingspan as long as Mutombo; however, the only thing Jason was good at was throwing back shots. The more Jason threw back, the angrier he got. Alcoholics referred to this type of drunk as an angry drunk. Jason had his reasons to be angry, but he wouldn't dare bring them up at the bar. Jason was roughly the size of Tiny—a bit slimmer around the waistline. He had a well-trimmed Van Dyke goatee that he had been wearing ever since high school. He liked to wear the color blue too, and not just any blue appropriate for a night out in town, but a bright royal blue. Jason told the girls he wore blue because it matched his eyes, which were brown, not blue.

Of all the locals who spent their entire evenings whistling and hollering and tossing bills at the girls, Jason was the one who had gotten under her skin the most during her stint as a dancer.

The girls called him a "*grabber.*"

After Jason had a few drinks, he liked to get touchy with people. Girl or guy, it made no difference to him. Several times the girls had let Tiny know about Mr. Feather Tickler. Tiny had warned Jason not to touch the girls again. This, however, had been the second warning he had given Jason; and we all know what happened with a third.

Three strikes and you're out.

The third time Jason touched one of the girls—Daisy was her name—Tiny had the night off. He did quite a number on her too. Left Daisy with a nice shiner, and he told Daisy if she ever told anybody about it, then he would kill her. Daisy never told Tiny, but she did tell Chloe.

When Chloe got wind of what Jay Bird was doing to the girls, including Daisy, she knew something had to be done.

And Chloe wasn't going to leave without saying goodbye.

That night, Jason Swight, a man who spent his evenings looking for trouble, a man who was known for using the only line he had in his bag of charms "Got a problem???" whenever someone had a bone to pick with him, a man who received pleasure in slapping around girls and treating them as if they were pieces of meat, a man who made *other* men look bad. . .

Well, that night, trouble found Jason.

Chloe marched into the nightclub, walked directly up to Jason, and gently whispered in his ear, "Now, it looks like you're the one with the problem. . ."

She didn't even have to look him directly in the eyes. All she needed was one glimpse.

She walked from the Flaming Eagle as Jason sat there on that same bar stool that he always sat on with a stupid expression on his face. She had turned everything to stone, except for his main organs as well as his flesh.

Everything else was left in a fixed state.

She didn't kill him, though.

That would be too easy.

Later that night, three bouncers helped Jason from the seat, his body forever stuck in a seated position, a gaping look on his stupid face.

From there, Chloe was left with one option, the *only* option she had been faced with ever since she left Whisperfront: Chloe had to run.

So, she found herself doing exactly that, running again.

———

AFTER Chloe left Louisiana, she found herself in a dilemma.

She had two directions: *north* or *west.*

North was Mississippi, unfinished business, and west was Anodes, a city Chloe was always curious about ever since she left Maine. She decided to travel west because the timing was *not* right. She could've easily paid him a visit, easily, but there was too much heat.

By the time she reached Arizona, after daily expenses, food and gas and whatnot, she was sitting on three thousand dollars. She made sure to avoid the big cities like Dallas and Albuquerque and Phoenix, and targeted the small towns. It was hard to find a decent job that would match as much as she earned at the Flaming Eagle.

So, she kept at it, moving from small town to small town until she found a nice refuge south of Flagstaff, Arizona—Anodes, Arizona.

There, Chloe picked up a more suitable job where she could keep her clothes on, and dance, of course, for fun, if she wanted to. The money was just as good, if not better than stripping; and Chloe received a free meal everyday.

Things were good for Chloe until the second Friday of February, Friday the Thirteenth, when the shit hit the fan. . .

ANODES, ARIZONA
FEBRUARY 13, 2015

CHLOE said her goodbyes to the co-owner of the diner, Phil, a man who had a body that was pushing obesity and a face that could pass as Marlon Brando's twin—in his *Dr. Moreau* days, that is—and left with her stomach full of today's house special, Momma's Rigatoni.

Chloe took three steps from Phil and Tony's—the third one done with the kick of her heel as she peeked down and checked the floppy, rabbit-eared shoelaces, making sure they were tied good and tight—when she heard the blistering sound of an engine rev from afar.

For only a split second, her confident strut came to a sudden halt (under a microscope: a scatterbrained woman who couldn't quite determine whether she was going forward or going backward, or in Chloe's case, going about her business or composing *a kill*.)

As Chloe proceeded forward, she rolled her eyes over her shoulder and noticed a car in the corner of her eye. A black Lincoln—an older model. Two men, Chloe spotted, wearing black shades. Definitely not from Anodes, and they certainly didn't have that pubescent astonishment like most tourists.

These two meant business.

The car followed Chloe another block down Main Street and parked next to the curb.

It was happening again, Chloe realized, *not* that thing, but the other. The thought alone stirred another feeling inside Chloe, richer, the relative of *that* oh-so dreadful feeling; but this time it wasn't another state of emptiness as she had felt before she rediscovered her troubling past, but rather the complete opposite. She couldn't help but wonder if it had something to do with the gaze. Whatever it was, she felt it like a dull ache in her bones, so deep as if she could actually cut it out and hold it in her palm, dripping with black slime or reeking of something foul like old dead fish.

A phantom of a smile flashed across one side of her face as she proceeded toward her apartment.

Chloe stopped at Used Reads, as she always did on the way home, and skimmed over the monthly periodicals on the bottom shelf of the rack. She started with FASHION and STYLE magazines and then moved her way to the ENTERTAINMENT section, rifling through each gaudy magazine until she crossed the familiar image of a debonair man.

Suddenly, she did a double take of the man.

Then, another feeling came over her, one of great distress.

She reached down and picked up the *Flashback* magazine.

Her eyes did not fool her.

On the cover was her father, Leon Dorsey. The photo was much older, from the early 80's—1984 to be exact.

In awe, Chloe read the caption to herself, "A Week With Mr. Hopkins."

She opened the magazine and turned to the article.

"Oh shit," were the first words to spill from her mouth.

As she skimmed through the article, she realized that everything from the USB flash drive had been written in the article, including Leon's upbringing, her *history*, her birth name, Jaelene Chloe Dorsey, what happened in Rural—the horrific massacre—what happened between Leon and the Company, as well as the chaos in Death Valley, even what recently happened in Whisperfront with the shocking discovery of the human remains, including the journalist, Renny Jacobson; all of it was in here for people to feast upon.

Without glancing over her shoulder at the Lincoln, she closed the magazine and kindly handed the clerk a twenty.

When he reached out to hand Chloe her change, she was already gone.

—

CHLOE decided to make a pit stop at the Internet café a couple of blocks away from her apartment.

Months had passed since Chloe had been on the Internet to google, surf, or most importantly, check her email; and since she had completely shut out the outside world after she managed to escape from Whisperfront in one piece, she didn't know exactly what was going on.

She found an open computer in the back of the café where it was fairly quiet.

As she went to type in her password, she drew a blank.

Could it be a *birth date* or a *favorite food* or *an album*?

Then, strangely, Chloe thought about her former employer, Universal Satellite Radio, what it felt like to work there—*that* fucking *hell*; and like that, the password came to Chloe. It happened to be the same as her USR login: ALCATRAZ123. Chloe typed in the password with expectancy, pressed the ENTER key, and shazam! She was in.

She scrolled through pages and pages of new email, at
least six pages from promotions, mostly spam, as well as
viruses from big-name retailers—child's play for even an
amateur hacker—to emails from the upper management
at USR.

She ignored them all and scrolled back to the first page
where she found an email from thejs@idiscover.com—a
couple of days old, she saw.

The subject: *Read.*

She opened the strange email.

In the body of the email:

They're onto you.

P.S. I never wanted things to go down like that between
your father and me. He was a good man. *Remember* that.

Wondering who sent the cryptic email (more than
likely, it was he, Diego,)—*it's got to be him*, she thought
out loud—Chloe looked around the café with a pale emptiness upon her face.

She moved her head around the computer's monitor
and then shot a glance outside the café.

It was there, that same black Lincoln, which had been
following her ever since she left the diner, parked along
the curb.

She drew her bright eyes toward the screen.

Below, there was a link:

recording34587mp3.wav

After another survey around the café, she clicked on the
link.

An audio player opened on the screen.

She found a pair of greasy headphones to the right of
the keyboard and put them on.

(*There was static over the recording.*)

MR. HOPKINS [DISTORTED]: *There. . . was. . .*

(MR. HOPKINS' *voice clears up.*)

. . . a young girl named Agatha. . . grew. . . up in a place called Alimos, Greece, east of the port city Pireas and south of Athens.

Chloe pressed the PAUSE button and thought about that one particular name, the name Agatha—it was the same name as the one before.

The head. . . Chloe resumed the recording and turned up the volume on the keyboard.

She listened to the entire recording—her eyes bulging after that one name rolled from Leon's tongue, the name, *Medusa.*

"Medusa," Chloe uttered.

RENNY [SHOCKED]: Impossible—
MR. HOPKINS: In the head, that's where her true powers lie.
RENNY: But how? It's not real. They're [STUTTERING] just myths, stories—
MR. HOPKINS: Stories have been handed down for many centuries, Renny. You're a writer. You should know that there is always some *truth* in a story, even in the fictional ones.

The recording suddenly stopped.

Stunned from the recent story, she removed the headphones from her ears.

She didn't think too much of the story, at least not until she arrived at her apartment.

In the meantime, Chloe highlighted page after page of email with the mouse and then dragged each highlighted page into the trash.

Her next two steps: clearing the bin and then deleting the email account.

After the account was deleted, she exited the Internet café in a timely manner.

—

CHLOE did four things after stepping out of the shower: first, she wiped the steam from the mirror and looked over her eyes and thought about how cool it was to finally—after all these years—make sense of the origin of how she came to be this way, but she tried not to let it all go to her head; second, she wrapped the towel around her breasts; third, she grabbed the USB flash drive from the cutout in the Holy Bible, the King James Version, and hid it in the side pouch of her purse; and fourth, she packed her belongings into a navy blue duffel bag.

She was halfway through packing when she suddenly heard a creaking sound from a footstep outside the doorway.

From the bed, both of Harley Jr.'s ears erected in curiosity, eyes opened wide and unblinking.

Chloe stopped what she was doing and listened closely to the outside noise, as did Harley Jr.

The creak slowly died out.

Another creak pierced through her ears—same with Harley Jr.'s—but this time the sound was drawn out in intervals like a held-in fart.

Chloe took one step into the hallway and glanced past the doorway.

Across the living room, she found two long shadows drifting across the narrow space underneath the front doorway.

There was a soft *click* and then a tense silence!

Chloe rushed back into the bedroom and grabbed the can of Zigzags from her purse.

As she popped open the can, the door was suddenly thrust open with the heel of a black boot, which caused Harley Jr. to pounce from the bed.

The two agents from Whisperfront, Agent Karp and Agent McClintock, stormed into the apartment with their stun guns drawn.

Harley Jr. charged at the two agents, but he was booted outside.

They checked the living room first, but she was nowhere to be found.

Next, they checked the hallway—Agent Karp leading the way.

The agent tiptoed into the hallway.

Halfway down, the agent's eyes were drawn to a shadow cast from behind the bathroom door. A rush of pain caused his head to tremble back and forth. The blood in his head went cold for a second and everything it touched turned staticky like a television, as if the nerves inside his body were being played like an old banjo.

Agent Karp shook away the fuzzy sensation and motioned to his partner, McClintock, who was now following close behind him.

The shadow shifted like a glitch on a television screen and then moved a little to the right, Agent Karp witnessed as he ambled toward the steamy bathroom on the far left.

The moment he arrived at the bathroom, he swung open the door but found nothing, no shadows, no Chloe, no movements, except for a towel swaying back and forth from the rush of air. What the agent failed to realize was that she had found his eyes the second he entered the hallway and traced them in the reflection of the hallway mirror.

In that tiny reflection, Chloe gazed the agent; however, the agent never turned to stone, as the gaze was known to do to people. Instead, she used the gaze the exact same way her father did while he assisted the Lansford Police Department. Except for that clerk in New Haven, the first time Chloe actually tried to get *inside* someone's head was not on a person but a stray cat she stumbled across in an alleyway or, better yet, a stray cat that had stumbled across her path. The results were catastrophic— and if she let what had happened to that stray cat get the best of her, she never would've recovered from the whole ordeal. As much as it tore her up inside, she knew there would be sacrifices, possibly brain damage or worse, death. That, Chloe knew. The image alone of the poor feline going berserk still haunted her: its chilling screech cutting through the alley like a baby's wail; and then, it clawing at its black eyes; and finally, it violently ramming the side of its head into the building until there was nothing left of its head but a bloody pulp.

As of now, Chloe had only two options: either deal with the card she had been dealt with or the other, the easy way out.

First, Agent Karp checked behind the shower curtain, but nobody was there, no shadow, no Chloe.

Then, he checked behind the door.

No shadows. No Chloe.

The air was still damp from the recent shower, which kept the agent on his toes. Even the vanity mirror, the agent noticed, was still cloudy from the warm steam.

Another sensation pounded against his veins. He focused his eyes on the mirror and kept them there until suddenly an invisible finger drew a smiley face on the mirror.

The agent rubbed the blur from his eyes and, as before, shook the tremble from his head.

"What's wrong?" Agent McClintock said from behind.

"Nothing," the agent said shortly. "It's nothing."

The two agents stepped back into the hallway.

One of them froze—Karp did. Beads of sweat raced down the sides of his forehead. His face fisted into a sharp grimace. The agent tried to fight off the stabbing pain, but his upper body was thrust forward. He grabbed his stomach and leaned into a hunched position.

"Karp?" Agent McClintock said as he tended to his partner.

"It's her..." Agent Karp groaned as he removed his bloody hands from his stomach, "...she's here..."

As Agent McClintock drew his eyes to his partner's hands (both of them, which were *not* covered in blood as

Agent Karp had imagined), he directed his attention toward the hallway and found Chloe standing inches away from him.

The white towel was stripped from her body. She was standing there naked, drenching wet from the recent shower. Her hazel eyes were wide and bright and drawn on the agent.

In return, the agent stared back at Chloe.

Before he could fire the stun gun, Chloe kneed Agent Karp in the face, pulled him upright, and used his body as a shield.

"Take the shot. . . " Agent Karp cried out.

Agent McClintock's face went blank, as Karp's did before. He moved the stun gun toward his partner's head and mindlessly fired a shot at Agent Karp, *not* Chloe. The two prongs went directly into his partner's forehead.

As he violently trembled from the voltage, Chloe grabbed his jaw with one hand and then the backside of his head with the other, and broke Agent Karp's neck with one swift motion!

His lifeless body flopped to the floor, but not before Chloe grabbed the stun gun from his loose grip and fired a shot at the other agent. The prongs hit the agent in the gut, but he quickly ripped out the prongs before he could feel the full effect of the shock. She used the wall as a spring and flipped over the agent, caught his arm before he could land a punch, and threw an uppercut to the backside of his elbow. The ulna in McClintock's forearm punctured directly through the skin of his forearm and protruded through his sleeve, which caused him to cry out in bloody horror. She didn't end there, though. She kneed Agent McClintock directly in the kidney, forcing his limp body to the side.

Now that the agent was left vulnerable, she grabbed a handful of his face and drove the side of it into the wall. The impact of the blow instantly knocked out the agent.

As the two agents now lay on the floor—one of them dead while the other one unconscious—Chloe searched them both. She came across a gun—a real one, not a stun gun—as well as their wallets. She opened the wallets; and then, after a shocking revelation, she realized that they were *not* FBI agents, as it stated on both of their badges.

Chloe peeled away the photos from their fake IDs, revealing the *real* Agent Karp and *real* Agent McClintock.

She removed the pistol from Agent McClintock's holster and placed it inside the duffel bag.

—

SHE didn't bother with a bra.

She threw on some skinny jeans and a black tee, which she tied in a knot around her waist side, and then slipped into a new pair of black boots that she bought with her money from work. She didn't bother with the shoelaces either.

When she stepped outside the apartment, she found Harley Jr. hobbling onto the steps. From the looks of him, he had broken his leg in the fall. Chloe picked up Harley Jr., provoking a sudden and yet soft-spoken howl from the dog. She carried him to her 2001 used Camry that she had bought after ditching the Sable in San Antonio. The Camry had over a hundred thousand miles and sputtered whenever she started it up; but nonetheless, it ran. She exited the parking lot and found the same black Lincoln that was following her earlier parked on the street.

She eased the Camry next to the black car and saw that nobody was inside.

As Chloe drove away, a sudden gunshot rang out!

The bullet hit the back windshield and struck the passenger seat next to her, nearly hitting Harley Jr. in the neck.

She shot a glance toward the rear view mirror and saw Agent McClintock lurching behind the car. One side of his face was masked in red blood. One of his arms was dangling like a soggy noodle. The other one—the good one— had a pistol aimed directly at Chloe's head.

She slammed the gear in reverse and hit the gas pedal.

The agent fired two more shots at Chloe.

Before he could fire another, she rammed the agent and sent him tumbling across the parking lot.

She stepped out of the car and noticed he was facedown. He wasn't moving a muscle; of course, that was the whole point.

Then, she got back into the Camry and drove away.

As Chloe sped down the open interstate—the vast desert on both sides of her—she manually rolled down the window and aired out her wet stringy hair. She checked the rear view once more, but didn't see any cars, mainly Lincolns, following her.

In that heightened moment of adrenaline, a smile found its way onto Chloe's face. It wasn't like any other smile she had felt before, at least not lately. The last time she remembered smiling this way was when things came naturally, like walking or talking. She was only a young girl at the time—seven or eight years old, she remembered. Although Chloe couldn't remember exactly where she was since her family traveled so much, Chloe was, for the most part, happy. For many years, as much as she yearned to feel that smile on her face, *to know that it was real*, Chloe never felt the smile on her face the same way she did as a young girl.

Now, she did.

And it was a good thing.

The best.

GORDON POINTE, MAINE
NOVEMBER 8, 2014

FROM a distance, the sight of the two strolling next to one another through the woods was enough to guarantee a double take and then perhaps a laugh.

Two weeks ago, when Larry "The Second" Hormel saw the two dogs exiting from the bushes—the little one clung to the big one's hind legs like a pup to its mother—Larry wasn't laughing. Not one bit. Larry Hormel—having owned dogs both big and small throughout his entire life—

knew the hurt in their eyes, for he had seen that same hurt in his own eyes not long ago. Larry wasn't a bright man by any means (at seventeen, he dropped out of high school and worked the double at the lumberyard in order to support himself and his mother who could no longer work due to a rare autoimmune disease), but Larry was brilliant when it came to reading things—human or non-human. He could look into a man's eyes and know everything about him. Momma Jo called it the Beat of God—a "thunderous pound in your chest whenever you see someone in need." She always said to Larry, "God didn't bless you with a brain, Ole Larry, the world has too many of them, but He sure did *bless* you, Ole Larry, with a heart of gold."

After Momma Jo passed in the spring of 1997, it was just Larry and his golden retriever, Chewy, named after Chewbacca from the movie, *Star Wars*. He had rescued Chewy at the shelter. Chewy's former master was what Larry called—in polite terms—*not* a nice man. Whenever Chewy would get out of line, his former master would dip Chewy's paws in hydrochloric acid. The damage was permanent, and the poor dog was left with four bare paws, which had been heavily scarred from the acidic burns. One rainy afternoon, a family had found the dog on the side of the road, holding up traffic, its raggedy coat caked with shit and mud. They took him in for a couple of days, let him stay in the garage, gave him food and shelter, and bathed him. Then, after they realized that the dog wouldn't be appropriate for the children, they dropped him off at the Humane Society, hoping that a person would pick him up.

That person was none other than Larry Hormel, who happened to be in the market for a new dog to give to Momma Jo. It was love at first bark. Momma Jo didn't care much for him at first. She was more of a lap cat lady.

Eventually, she came around.

Then, on a warm, muggy night last summer, Larry was woken up in the dead of night by the sudden yowl of his beloved dog. When he went to check on Chewy, he was already dead. Heart murmur, the vet told him.

Larry figured the best way to get over Chewy's death was to get back out there—hunting, that is—with or without his best friend; otherwise, he might never hunt again.

So, initially, he was hesitant to take in both Smiley and Biscuit, for there was *still* a gaping hole left inside him that no human or dog could fill—and that gaping hole, Larry knew, would be there forever. Larry would have to learn how to live with it because that was what Momma Jo had preached to him—but when the two ran to Larry with wagging tails and smiles on their faces, Larry couldn't refuse. Stranger or no stranger, they darted toward Larry the moment they saw him trudging through the grove with a rifle rested over his right shoulder, two dead ducks in his left hand.

In the days that followed, Larry searched for the owner; and then, after the news about the two dogs spread around town, he learned of their owner's apparent suicide.

A week later, Larry had himself two new hunting buddies, although the little one couldn't hunt worth a damn. Smiley, on the other hand, was born a hunter, a hunter's hunter.

In the days ahead, both Larry and Smiley came across a hidden gem right outside Pirate's Cove called Gordon Pointe.

Three miles inland, the wooded land opened up into a beige-colored field covered with waist-high weeds and a dale with a river. The river fingered out into three other brooks. It was Smiley who actually found the spot, *not* Larry.

For Larry and Smiley, it was a hunter's wet dream.

Since they had a lot of luck last week (they brought home seven good-sized mergansers—the law during season was that they could only carry five, but Larry got away with an extra one or two), they decided to pay one last visit to the Pointe before the cold weather plumped its fat derrière over Maine.

As soon as Larry and Smiley started wandering through a trail in the woods, Smiley paused and sniffed the cool air. Its front paw cocked ever so slightly.

Then, it took off down another trail. . .

"Smiley!' Larry yelled out. "Where ya goin', boy?"

Larry secured his rifle and then chased after the dog. He ran about a quarter of a mile before he found the dog digging his paws into a loose mound of dirt.

Larry asked, "Whatcha got there, Smiley?"

Smiley drove his snout into the ground and then, again, clawed his paws over the loose dirt.

Larry kneeled down next to Smiley. He too got involved in the action as well and began to scatter away the dirt.

After two initial sweeps, the dirt, he saw, started to move and come alive.

Then, the two finally came across something unnatural, a royal blue tarp underneath the dirt.

Larry eased the dog aside and peeled away the tarp, revealing an entire layer of maggots.

He flinched from the sight of the maggots as well as the smell, which was strong enough to knock over a bucking bull.

The smell was horrendous, but he knew all too well what the smell was. Unlike Smiley's previous master, he had never gotten used to that smell, the smell of death.

He pulled back on the tarp until it revealed a human arm. The body had been dead for a couple of weeks, Larry knew, and it was approaching the latter stages of decay when nothing was left of the human remains but skull and bones.

JESTER, MISSOURI
FEBRUARY 16, 2015

"RISE and shine, Mr. D-Man," Luke chirped as the bright sunrays forced Merrotti to shade his disfigured face. Luke moved his way to the other window and slid open the blinds, bringing forth more light into the room. "I hope you got a lot of rest last night because," he said over his shoulder as he opened the last set of blinds, "if you didn't, I promise you will tonight."

Luke grabbed the wheelchair from the bathroom and wheeled it over to the hospital bed.

He noticed a photograph in Merrotti's badly scarred hand.

"What do you got there, D-Man?" Luke asked Merrotti.

Merrotti didn't answer, of course, couldn't.

"You mind?" Luke said curiously, as he pried the photograph from Merrotti's hand. "Let's see what we got here. . ."

Luke looked down at the photograph. The edges of it were burned, but the people in the picture were *still* intact. He asked Merrotti who the bald dude was in the picture—"Mr. Clean," Luke called him—*the butler*, that is (the other two, the maid and the nurse, Luke didn't ask about).

Luke asked once more, but the detective didn't answer, of course, couldn't.

RUBIO, VENEZUELA
MARCH 19, 2015

A motorcade of black unmarked vehicles equipped with bulletproof windows pulled up behind an open market located in San Nicolasa.

An entourage of men in black suits stepped from the vehicles and escorted the President of the United States, President Robert Shaw, through a grungy alleyway behind a café. The entire place was run-down. Most of the foul smell had come from the meat stall next to the café, which had been cleared out prior to the President's entrance, even the employees who worked there.

At the bar in the corner of the café sat Diego. He was sipping from an espresso and playing it cool and casual. He was dressed like the night: black suit that had been tailored by a local seamstress, black silk shirt, black tie, black leather knee high boots, which were waxed to a mirror shine, and a black leather glove, just one, *not* two, which he wore only on his immobile left hand.

Three secret service agents entered first.

Once they gave the "all clear" sign, the President finally entered the café.

"You look much shorter in person," Diego said from the bar, keeping to his cool composure.

"I didn't come here to small talk with some spic," President Shaw returned and then sat down at the wooden table in the middle of the room.

Four secret service agents surrounded President Shaw, two on each side.

The President pointed at the chair on the other end of the table, "Well, what are you waiting for?"

Diego took his time and finished his espresso.

Finally, he grabbed a camel-colored leather tote bag from the stool beside him and sat down in the chair directly across from the President.

Casual in manner, he carefully placed the tote bag on the table.

"First," the President said, "I want to know that it works before I buy."

"Of course," Diego returned casually. "Why would I sell you a product that doesn't work?"

President Shaw replied, "You'd be surprised. The Chinese do it all the time. . . "

"I assure you," Diego said. "It works."

"Good," he said hesitantly.

"May I ask why?"

"Why?"

"*Yes*," Diego said, sternly now. "Why?"

"I'm afraid the American people are beginning to lose ah. . . " the President paused for a moment, ". . . hope. They're losing hope in their government, as well as the men and women who protect them from slime like you."

"And that's what you're doing, looking after them?"

"It's my duty," President Shaw said, lacing his fingers on the table. "Now, it is time to convince the American people that sometimes *change* is the only answer for long-term stability." He turned his shoulder and shouted out, "Bring him in!"

Two more secret service agents entered the café, now making it six against one. They were carrying a local who was a couple of years older than Diego. The local, bug-eyed from the drugs they had been feeding him, was looking around the café as if it was the size of a mansion compared to the grubby hovel he had been living in for weeks. He had a swollen right eye that smelled of infection. He struggled a bit, but the two agents had a firm grip around his arms.

"What is this?" Diego said and suddenly stood from the chair.

"Relax, Mr. Tovar," the President said to Diego. "This here is Emilio. We found the mute, along with a couple of *rebeldes*, who tried to take out an associate of ours a couple of weeks ago. Oh!" the President cracked a smile, crooked like a seesaw. "Not to mention, the cute *chica* parked outside. You planning a quick getaway, Mr. Tovar?" He leaned forward over the table, eyes narrowing. "Now, I could care less what you filthy little people do in your filthy little country. However. . . Mr. Tovar, when it comes to messing with our money, we have a serious problem. I mean serious, *hombre*."

"The feeling is mutual, Mr. President," Diego said and nodded at Emilio. Their eyes sharpened, both Diego and Emilio. "I ask you to release this man here. In return, you can use me as one of your guinea pigs."

"You'd risk your life for a man you don't even know?"

"*Sí* (Yes)," Diego said.

"Nice try," the President said and then motioned to the secret service agent behind Diego.

The agent pulled out a pistol and placed the barrel behind Diego's head.

Grimacing, Diego raised his arms in the air—his left arm being much tougher to lift.

"Go ahead, Mr. Tovar," the President said. "Show me. . ."

Diego made an attempt toward the tote bag.

"Slowly!" President Shaw blurted out.

He was slow to open the bag. Carefully, he pulled out a glass jar. Inside the jar was Agatha's severed head. It looked the same as it did in Whisperfront: gray, scaly, and emaciated.

Next, Diego opened the jar, releasing a strong odor from inside.

A couple of agents covered their noses in disgust.

Diego plucked a scale, which was roughly the size of a fingernail, from her left cheek. He placed the glass jar over the head, sealed it tight, and then carefully placed the jar back inside the tote bag.

"Now, do it..." President Shaw said. "Convince this piece of shit to get on his knees and bark like a dog."

Diego furrowed his brows.

"You know..." the President turned to one of the agents. "How do you say dog in Spanish?"

"*Perro* (Dog)," the agent said.

He turned back around to Diego.

"Bark like a *perro*," President Shaw commanded. "Do it!"

"Mr. President," one of the agents said from behind. "Sir, I don't think that would be a good idea."

"Nonsense," he said callously. "I didn't come all the way out here in this cesspool for nothing. I want to see it work with my own eyes."

Diego was hesitant at first.

The President seethed, "I said 'Do it' goddamn it! That's an order!"

The agent behind Diego cocked the hammer.

"Okay," Diego said.

As Diego placed the scale on the back of his tongue, an agent, who was now wearing a visor, handed President Shaw a visor as well and advised him to wear it.

He asked, "How do I work this damn thing?"

The agent replied, "Just slip it on over the ears like so."

"That's it?"

"Correct."

The President slipped on the visor.

The remaining agents followed suit and slipped on their visors as well.

Diego exaggerated the swallow of the scale, scowling after it was ingested.

He opened his mouth and displayed his tongue, which was without the scale.

"Now, let's see you work your magic, Mr. Tovar," President Shaw said as he stepped away from the local man.

As Diego stood in front of the local man, Emilio (both eyes sharp and menacing), he bowed his head into a subtle nod and then. . . a wink. . .

The President, as well as the agents, didn't pick up on the gesture, but Emilio did.

In return, he nodded at Diego, as Diego before, subtly.

Suddenly, Diego swung his left arm around and smashed the agent's visor.

The blow cut right through the visor and shattered half of the agent's face. He spat out the scale from underneath his tongue while Emilio pulled himself away from one of the agents.

Diego yanked the pistol from the injured agent's hand.

While doing so, the pistol accidentally went off and shot Diego in the gloved hand. The bullet remarkably ricocheted from his hand and hit the agent in the leg.

The baffled agent cried out, but not for too long.

Diego fired two bullets into the agent's chest—instantly killing him—and then fired three more into the other agent grabbing Emilio.

After the two agents were taken care of—now leaving four of them left—Emilio finished off the agent with a stiff knee to his face followed by several vicious open hand jabs to the nose.

Three agents left.

Two agents fired at Diego, but Diego quickly rolled out of the way and shot one of the agents.

Emilio shot the other agent.

Now, two left.

One agent.

One President.

In a matter of seconds, Diego and Emilio ended up doing the same to the remaining agent who was guarding
the President and shot him dead.

Now, one person remained, President Robert Shaw,
who was cowered underneath the table with his hands
covering his ears.

Diego strolled toward the quivering President and removed the visor from his face.

"Please," President Shaw begged to Diego, "you'll never
get away with this. . . "

Diego aimed the pistol at the President's head and said
as he towered above, "*Esto es para todas las personas ino-
centes que has asesinado.*"

Then, President Shaw screamed, "I'm the President of
the United States, goddamn it!"

Composed, Diego relied, "Not anymore. . . "

He squeezed the trigger, shot the President directly between the eyes; and then, after he watched the blood
trickle from the wound, he hurried to Emilio, who was
clutching his shoulder.

"*¿Está herido* (Are you hurt)?"

He responded with sign language, a simple index and
middle finger closing against his thumb while shaking his
head *no*.

Next, Emilio spread out his hand—all five fingers held
outward—and pressed his thumb against his chest, which
meant fine.

(*No. Estoy bien*)

Diego examined Emilio for further injuries.

He noticed from a quick study that the bullet had gone
in and come out the other side.

"*Salgamos de aquí* (Let's get out of here)," Diego said as
he wrapped his arm around Emilio.

On the way out, Diego grabbed the tote bag from the
table.

The two amigos exited the bloodstained café.

Most of the locals in the town fled to their homes during
the gunfight.

Those valiant enough to see what the fuss was all about poked their heads from behind the shutters of their own windows and watched the local hero, "The Voice," escape down Main Street.

Diego and Emilio trekked up a hill along the sidewalk until they reached a rusty hatchback parked alongside the curb.

Outside the car they observed another secret service agent, dead like the others.

He took a knife to the throat and had bled out over the street.

Inside the parked car, Sophia was sitting behind the steering wheel.

She reached around the seat and opened the back door for Diego.

"*Entrar* (Enter)!" she cried out. "*Apurate* (Hurry)!"

Diego helped Emilio into the backseat.

Then, he sat down next to Emilio, placed the tote bag next to the February Issue of *Flashback* that was wedged in the middle of the seat, and closed the door behind him.

He tapped Sophia on the shoulder and said to her, "*Vamonos* (Let's go)."

As they drove toward the mountains, he turned to his amigo, his good friend, Emilio.

He said to him, "*Todo el mundo estará después de nosotros para lo que poseemos* (Everyone will be after us for what we possess)."

Emilio raised his hand and balled it into a fist—his hand acting like his head—and then moved his fist up and down.

(*Sí*)

Diego grabbed Emilio's fist with both of his hands and said, "*Dos contra el mundo* (Two against the world)."

Then, Emilio repeated: first, he held up two fingers, which represented the number *two*; second, with a flat hand, he pressed the tip of his right hand against his open left palm, which was flat as well, *against*; and third, he ended with the sign for *world*, which was with both hands in the shape of a W, and then, simultaneously, moved both hands (his right hand moving forward and his left moving backward) over one another in a circular motion.

(*Dos contra el mundo*)

A laugh surprisingly leaped from Diego's mouth.

He patted Emilio over his knee, smiled, and said to him, "*Dos contra el mundo.*"

PART ONE
THE PALE GIRLS

ON the set of director Van Nostrum's latest political thriller, *Bulletheart* (2015), screenplay by D.L. Dumar:

EXT. CASABLANCA, MOROCCO - HASSAN II MOSQUE - DAY

The sky is overcast, the blurry pink sun still climbing from the horizon. The weather is calm, though, except for an ocean breeze whistling through the air.

A ray of sunlight lances through thick, dark clouds and shines over the minaret.

MADI and ANTIGO stand against the railing of a balcony, the minaret towering behind them.

                    ANTIGO (O.S.)
          Nice day.

MADI doesn't move her eyes from the North Atlantic, waves crashing below. Her hand below clutches OMAR'S black bandana.

                    ANTIGO (CONT'D)
          Say, did I ever tell you the story
          about the chicken?

                    MADI
          I don't think so.

                          ANTIGO
          My father, he used to have this
          chicken coop. Every morning, he'd
          let Omar and I feed the chickens.
          Omar liked feeding the chickens.
          That was sort of his thing. Mine
          was making sure Omar did it cor-
          rectly. He did. There was this
          one little chicken in the flock. A
          runt named was Pepé. My father
          named it after the American cartoon
          character, Pepé Le Pew.

MADI furrows her brows. She has no words to say.

                      ANTIGO (CONT.)
          Ring a bell?

                          MADI
          Where exactly are you going with
          this, Antigo?

                          ANTIGO
          Pepé was a skunk with a French ac-
          cent, and Pepé was always chasing
          after this female skunk that was
          actually a black cat with white
          stripes. But Pepé was unaware of
          the cat because he was *blinded* by
          love.
              (lowers his head with a
            smile)
          I don't know why my father named
          this one chicken Pepé. He didn't
          smell like a skunk to me. *Perhaps*
          Pepé did to the other chickens. I
          don't know. Perhaps that was why
          they never went near him.

MADI pulls herself from the railing. She looks ANTIGO
in the eyes and gives him *the look*. Head lowered,
eyes sharp, the expression almost adolescent. ANTIGO
shrugs off the look -- hates it.

                          MADI
              (eyes glazing over)
          Antigo? Please. Don't do this to
          me. Not now.

ANTIGO
Anyway, Pepé, he was the smallest
chicken in the flock. The runt,
you know, just like Omar. He certainly wasn't chasing after any
other chickens or animals pretending to be chickens. Every time we
saw Pepé, he was always alone in
the corner of the coop. The others
in the flock kept their distance
from little Pepé until one day another chicken, twice as big as
Pepé. My father named him Bill after President William Taft.

MADI
Your father has an interesting way
of selecting names.

ANTIGO
(bobbing his head, smiling
again)
He did. So, one day, Bill decided
to venture away from the flock and
approach little Pepé. Pepé wanted
nothing to do with Bill, but Bill
kept antagonizing Pepé. Then, out
of nowhere, little Pepé attacked
Bill. It wasn't much of a fight.
Pepé broke both of Bill's legs. My
father told us there was nothing
that could be done to help the
chicken. We had to put it down.

MADI
Did you at least eat the chicken?

ANTIGO
Of course. Best chicken ever.

ANTIGO laughs -- a half laugh. MADI keeps her rever-
ent composure.

MADI
Antigo, what's your point?

ANTIGO
Afterwards, the other chickens ac-
cepted little Pepé into the flock.
My father loved Pepé so much that

> he decided to keep Pepé as a pet.
> Omar was Pepé, Madi, that lonely,
> frightened chicken that no other
> chicken would go near. Like Pepé,
> Omar always wanted to fit in with
> the others. But he was never like
> them, not until he met you. Madi,
> you gave him a reason to fight for
> something greater than anything on
> this earth. You showed my brother
> that there was nothing. . .
>> (a passion burning in his
>> eyes)
> . . . I mean, *nothing*, wrong with
> being on the outside. Omar. . . he
> didn't have to prove anything to
> anybody, Madi. Only you. Because
> he loved you so much, and the seed
> Omar planted will one day blossom
> into something beautiful.

He places his hand over MADI'S. Her watery eyes move toward his.

> ANTIGO (CONT'D)
> Madi, you showed my brother that he
> didn't have to be like the rest of
> them.

The tears fall from MADI'S eyes -- a stream of tears.

> ANTIGO (CONT'D)
> We are *all* like chickens in a coop,
> waiting to die. The question,
> Madi: 'When will our own Bill rise
> to the occasion and test our fate?'
> When, or if that time comes, will
> we fight like Omar did or will we
> die?

> FADE TO BLACK.

A raspy voice off screen yelled, "Cut!"

Van climbed from his red director's chair—*the throne*, as producers called it—and walked onto the set.

He said to both the actors and the crew, "That is a wrap, ladies and gentlemen!"

The flamboyant director had a bushy beard that was turning gray and a kangaroo pouch for a belly; and he was dressed as if he was about to go on an African safari. Those who knew him well called him Nanny, and those who were new to work with Van called him Mr. Nostrum. He liked the word *mister* in front of his name. Van thought it made him sound respectable. He wore the same outfit while filming: the Safari getup, that smelly, sweat-stained New York Yankees baseball cap, which used to be black, but now it was faded to the color blue, and Aviators with an orange tint (even during the night-time, Van never took them off).

Van approached the two actors, Antigo, who was played by the up and coming actor, Hugo Minstry, and Madi, played the great Kaia Ganguly.

Makeup, wardrobe, and a couple other people who had flown to watch the final shoot tagged along as well.

Relief poured from the actors' faces, mainly Kaia's.

"Incredible, Kaia," Van said jubilantly and hugged Kaia.

"Thanks, Nanny..." Kaia said over Van's shoulder, the relief pouring from her strained voice.

"Why don't you take five and then, when you're done, we'll take some pictures together."

Kaia sighed.

"I'm a mess, Van," she uttered.

The director rubbed Kaia on the shoulder.

"Take as long as you want, dear," Van said to her. "You've earned it."

Kaia smiled, holding back the tears—the real ones.

"*Aw,*" she said. "Thank you, Van. Seriously."

—

As she made her way to her trailer, she received a round of handshakes and hugs from both producers and writers alike.

Her trailer was home away from home. Kaia got the trailer back in 2001, which seemed like yesterday, when she landed a supporting role next to the fabulous James Parker on the Hollywood blockbuster, *Hunter Down*, a shoot 'em up flick that had its success in the box office for two weeks until it was replaced with a remake of *Planet of the Apes*. For the next six years, Kaia landed roles in other Hollywood blockbusters (however, none of them were as big as *Hunter Down*). By 2008, Kaia was *so* yesterday. She was just another old face among new ones. Kaia was still gorgeous—a nine or ten to a bachelor's standards—but she knew down to her bones that she couldn't compete with the younger actors.

Unlike the newbies, Kaia had worked her way from the bottom to the top. She was a runner for about a year and a half, mostly fetching coffee for some prima donna or some wannabe producer who didn't do shit. After that, she starred as an extra in several TV pilots, remakes, and spin-offs that went straight to the graveyard in Studio B where bad ideas go to die. There had been countless times she wanted to hang it up, but whatever adversities were thrown her way, Kaia stuck with it. *Never* did she blow or fuck her way to the top. Kaia was a classy lady, one of the hardest working actresses in the business, but she flew under the radar throughout most of her career.

Eventually, Hollywood abandoned the natural look and went with a modern and yet mainstream approach in casting actors: fake tits and Barbie doll faces and an actor who wasn't afraid to show a little skin for the camera. The dramatic shift disgusted Kaia so much that she left Los Angeles for good. Never looked back. Not once. Kaia kept her trailer, though. In other words: Eat shit, you fake-ass bitches! You can have all of my rights, but you can't take my trailer.

For the next couple of years, Kaia did a little soul searching and traveled back to her hometown in India. She ended up getting a new agent, who got her some gigs in Bollywood. She did that for about two years until around 2012 when independent filmmaking was starting to make some noise in the industry. She chose to focus more on indie films. These films didn't make a lot of money in the box office (most, if not all of them, played at small art houses scattered around the country), not like Hollywood blockbusters.

And, of course, she kept the trailer too.

It was like any other fourteen-year-old trailer: a queen size bed, kitchen, and a lounging area with a couch.

Kaia had shared many memories in this trailer.

Some good, while others bad.

—

AFTER Kaia disrobed, she removed her makeup in front of the vanity mirror.

There was a knock on the door.

"Kaia," a woman said from outside the trailer.

Kaia heard the name, but didn't respond.

The name was said again and then again until Kaia heard the name *Madi*.

She turned away from the mirror.

"Yes," she said.

"Kaia," her agent returned, "can I come in?"

Kaia, she thought.

The name sounded strange to Kaia at first. She thought the name was hers. But, of course, she thought. It was hers.

She snapped from her daze and then finally said, "Yeah."

The wobbly door squeaked open.

Kaia's agent, Penelope, short in stature with a cute stub of a nose, stood at the top step with her arms folded over her chest.

She asked Kaia, "How you feel?"

"Good," Kaia said abruptly. Then, her voice dropped like an anchor. "A little sad."

"Me too," Penelope replied and closed the door behind her. "What a shoot! I wish it would never end, but, you know. . ."

"Eventually, you have to say goodbye. Right?"

"That's right."

Penelope cracked a smile.

Kaia placed the damp towel on the edge of the counter and stared into the mirror.

Penelope stepped closer.

"Are you sure everything's okay?"

"I. . ."

"What is it, Kaia?"

"Forget about it."

She grabbed the towel and proceeded to remove the dark eye shadow from her face. She only got through one eye before she stopped. Again, she stared into the mirror as if she didn't know the woman who was staring back at her—a stranger.

"Kaia?"

"I. . ."

"You can tell me."

"I don't think I can do this anymore, Penelope."

"Right." Her agent rolled her eyes, but Kaia never caught the foolish gesture. "How many times have I heard *that one* before?"

"I'm serious this time, Penelope," Kaia said as she placed the damp towel aside. "Look at me. I'm not getting any younger, Penelope. I am thirty-four years old, which, in this profession, means I should find something else to do."

"What are you talking about?" Penelope said fiercely as she crossed her arms. "Come on, Kaia. You're doing great. *We're* doing great. I got literally ten scripts in my office, all waiting to be read, and they're gems, Kaia. All of them. *Gems.*"

"When have you ever stopped to think about what I want, Penelope?" she asked. "It's all about *you*. What if I want a life? Have you ever thought about that?"

Deflated, Penelope said, "Acting is your life, Kaia."

"It's not!" Kaia cried out and suddenly bolted from her chair. "This isn't a fucking life! I mean, what the hell am I doing here, Penelope? Really? I'm living in a goddamn fantasy world!"

"Get yourself together, Kaia," Penelope said flatly and then opened the trailer door. "You and I both know that the last day on set is always the hardest. Let go, Kaia. *Let go.*"

MARSEILLE, FRANCE
MARCH 28, 2015

AT the Clinique Saint Marc—a prestigious mental hospital two blocks from the Bassin de Radoub on the Mediterranean Sea—there was a particular patient who received most of the attention, not because of her condition, but because of who she was. That patient's name was Juliet Baudin, and she was the daughter of the notorious international model turned philanthropist, Avril Baudin. Juliet was twenty-seven years old, and she once shared the same beauty as her mother. Three years ago, Juliet moved back into her mother's cottage in the countryside of Nantes from the States—Juliet was attending one of the top schools in Boston where she was studying to become a veterinarian but later dropped out due to personal reasons. Her mother, Avril, considered one of the first black models in France who made it big in the States during the mid Eighties, was now well into her fifties and, instead of modeling gigs, she used her beauty to advertise beauty products in TV commercials—hand lotions and hair products and whatnot. Avril did that for a while until the accident.

A year after her daughter came home from school, Juliet's condition worsened.

One afternoon, Juliet attacked her mother with a pan of piping hot oil, which left Avril scarred with first degree burns on the side of her neck, as well as the lower part of her face. Eventually, Avril's acting career was cut short, and she had no other choice than to check her daughter into Clinique Saint Marc.

As she did once a week, she paid a visit to Juliet—same time, same day, which was on a Thursday.

When Avril entered the room, her daughter didn't budge, not even flinch. The room was fairly empty, except for a bed and a desk, which took up very little space. On the desk was a box of crayons, which were scattered every which way—the color red being her daughter's favorite color. Without the desk, the room could've easily passed as another prison cell, but Avril learned through lots of research that Clinique Saint Marc had the best doctors in the country.

She stopped by the desk and skimmed over the doodling that her daughter had been currently working on, each one sketched with black and red crayons. The doodling was disturbing, one in particular: a sketch of a woman with hair like snakes, streaks of red bolting from her gaping black mouth—Avril later learned that these were what her daughter called her *doodies*, which was a cross between a doodle and a selfie, basically, a self portrait of one's self. The thought alone of her daughter imagining herself looking this way—like this grotesque, demonic-like creature—had sickened Avril the most.

She glanced at her daughter, who was still lying in the same position when she entered the room: resting on her back, both eyes staring vacantly at the ceiling.

"Hello, Juliet," Avril said carefully as she ambled toward the bed.

She pulled up a chair and sat next to Juliet, who, as before, didn't budge an inch. Juliet had blue eyes like her father and dark skin like her mother. The features on her face appeared as if an artist with bad proportion had drawn them in a rush. Her nose was tall, very distinctive, and it ran all the way up to the bridge of her brow; and her chin was alien-like, long and pointy. Her mother had asked her to try modeling. She had the look: pretty and thin, distinct. Now, she wasn't pretty. She had long scars next to her eyes and mountainous ridges along what used to be the smooth and round structure of her cheeks. And Juliet wasn't thin either. Ever since she checked into Clinique Saint Marc, Juliet had put on fifty plus pounds. She ate three square meals a day; and yet the only time she burned off the calories was when she lifted a crayon to draw, or, in her case, to doodle.

Avril's eyes traced down to Juliet's wrists, which were both fastened to the railing of the bed.

"I'm going to find a way to get you out of here," Avril said as she stroked her daughter's forehead. Juliet's eyes remained still, vacant. "We're going to get you better, Juliet, and you'll come back home where you belong. Okay?" She combed her daughter's greasy hair around the edge of her ear. "I miss you, Juliet," she said to Juliet. "Rose misses you." She cleared the tears from her eyes. They always came. Always. The tears. Even if Avril promised herself that today would be the day she would not cry, she would always break that promise. *Always.* She took a deep breath through her nose, exhaled through her mouth, and said to Juliet, "She sits by the doorway every afternoon, waiting for you to come home."

Juliet robotically turned her head toward her mother and vacantly stared at her.

Both of Juliet's eyes were dull and droopy. Juliet had saggy bags under her eyes as well, from all of the medications she had been taking.

Avril stared back into her eyes and saw nothing—like the soul had been reduced to a spec of dirt.

"I love you, Juliet, I love you so much," Avril said, but then Juliet turned away and stared back at the ceiling.

—

OUTSIDE the room stood Avril, as well as her doctor, Doctor Albert.

Avril asked Doctor Albert, "*Les restrictions nécessaires, docteur* (Are the restraints necessary, doctor)?"

"*Oui* (Yes)."

"*S'il vous plait* (Please). . ."

"*Je suis désolé, Avril* (I'm sorry, Avril)," Doctor Albert said to Avril. "*C'est pour son bien* (It's for her own good)."

SEATTLE, WASHINGTON
APRIL 2, 2015

COREY was twenty-six when his mother, Carolyn Fiddle, unexpectedly passed away from an aneurysm in 2010. At the time, Sally was still a baby—just over twelve months. Corey and his daughter didn't have to worry about personal finances for a very, very long time after he received the money that was left behind from his mother's small fortune, which had always remained a mystery to him because his mother never worked a single day in her life. Not one, he remembered. There was one time Carolyn had talked about the money to her son, when he was old enough to wipe on his own and curious enough to ask about his heritage. Carolyn told her son that she received a "kind" settlement from his birth father. Corey never met his birth father. There was Richard—or *Richie*—who helped raise Corey throughout his childhood. Then, after Richie pulled the greatest trick known to man—even the wondrous Houdini would've been impressed by the disappearing act—there were other men: some who came and went as they pleased, some who came at strange hours of the day, and others who lingered for a few days. Corey had forgotten their names, most of them. Didn't care for them, except for Brad, the guy who played the charming and yet diabolical Doctor Stan Crain on the short-lived soap opera series *From Where We Fall*. And that was that. . . Not once did Corey ever ask his mother any questions about his father or who he was or what he did for a living or, most importantly, *where* he was. Was he pals with Houdini as well?

To Corey, his father was dead.

After his mother died, Corey and his daughter moved into the two-story house that his mother had left behind for him and her six-year-old granddaughter.

Since Corey was separated (three years ago, his ex-wife tried several times to build a case against Corey, saying that he was an abusive person and didn't deserve custody over Sally, called the cops on several occasions, reporting that he hit her when, in fact, he hadn't laid a hand on her, he wasn't the type; in other words, the woman was a bat-shit crazy bitch), the house was more than enough room for the two, but it had its advantages.

A year ago, Corey did a complete makeover on the house to please Sally, who, at the age of three, was diagnosed with having a mild case of Asperger's Syndrome. For two months, he filled his head with reading material on Asperger's from A to Z—even down to the science. He decided to remove all chemicals from the house, including cleaning supplies; he even switched Sally's diet to strictly organic, no red meat or processed foods either—"The way food was intended to be eaten," he said. Lastly, Corey changed the silverware to plastic utensils. It had dawned on him last year that his daughter was not fond of silverware, especially the sound of it. He assumed that switching to natural products could help her in the long run. Corey always wondered if it had been brought on from the environment or other factors like pollution or pesticides or Wi-Fi. The real culprit, he realized, was silverware. Not the environment. Not even chemicals, but *silverware*. It wasn't the feel of it. It was the sound of it, when he cleaned it or loaded or unloaded it from the dishwasher. That clinking sound of silverware drove Sally into what Corey called "fits." At times, the fits were violent. He had scars on his arms and back to prove it. Other times, they were dangerously close to mental breakdowns—Sally would cover her ears and curl up into a fetal position. Corey spent months searching for an answer, in his books, on YouTube videos, or talking to other parents who had children with Asperger's, anything to set his mind at ease. Sally saw over a dozen doctors, but none of them had a diagnosis for her. That was when Sally's father decided to make the *change* on his own.

After he cleared the table of dirty dishes—all biodegradable—which went directly into the trashcan, Corey went to check on Sally whose room was upstairs. He knocked twice on the door before entering.

Sally was sitting on the end of her bed, staring at the many stoned statuettes on the shelves that her father constructed for her. And painted for her too. Sally's choice: red, but not just any red, crimson red. She had all sorts of statuettes ranging from rabbits to squirrels, all of them done with exceptional detail, life-like. Whenever Corey asked his daughter where she had gotten these statuettes, she would tell him in the forest in the backyard.

Next to the shelves was another shelf, a smaller wooden one that Corey had also built and painted for Sally.

On the red shelf were his daughter's books—mostly *Doctor Seuss* books—which Corey enjoyed reading to her right before he tucked her into bed and said goodnight. He sat down next to Sally on the bed.

"You know," Corey said to Sally, "I was thinking maybe we could go to the park. It's nice out. What do you say?"

Sally shrugged her shoulders, her eyes fixated on a stoned frog in her hand. Corey leaned in closer.

"You can bring him too."

"I don't like the park."

"We can go to the playground."

Again, Sally shrugged her shoulders.

"I tell you what," he said, "if we go to the park, I'll take you out for ice cream afterwards. How does that sound?"

"I don't wanna go," she pouted.

"Sally," Corey said and then let out a sigh, not big, but small enough to relieve the tightness in his chest. "I'm just trying to help here. There will be other kids your age you can play with."

"But I don't wanna play with them."

"*Please*, Sally," he said and tilted his head into Sally's range of vision. "For me. Can you do it for me?"

He stared into his daughter's eyes.

Finally, she nodded.

"Great," Corey said with a smile.

Sally stared back at the frog in her hands.

"I'll grab your shoes," he said as he stood up from the bed.

"Okay," Sally drawled.

—

COREY was sitting on a bench in Beatty Davis Park, watching his daughter play with her statuettes in the sand when a strange man dressed in a flannel shirt and green baseball cap approached him from behind.

"May I?" he said from Corey's side and pointed at the opposite end of the bench.

Corey turned toward the other end of the bench.

"Sure," he said after a quick study. "Be my guest."

The strange man placed a smartphone right beside him—an *unusual phone*, Corey saw in the corner of his eye, one that he had never seen before. There was no brand name on the phone. No labels. Just sleek and black with a touch screen on the front face.

"So," the stranger said with a nod, "which one is yours?"

Corcy pointed to Sally, the one in the orange tee and overalls.

He said, "That little angel right there."

"*Ah*," the stranger said as he acknowledged Sally. "She looks precious. So, what's her name?"

"Sally," Corey said. "Her name is Sally."

Corey studied the stranger, his manner, mainly his eyes.

"And you?" Corey said. "Do you have any children?"

"Lord no," he said exhaustedly over a long pause. He turned his shoulder and nodded at a beauty salon at the end of the strip mall across the park. "Waiting for the wife. She's currently getting one of those thingies done to her nails. You know ah. . . "

"A manicure?"

"That's it." He turned back around to Corey. "I know what you're thinking: Why in the hell did she drag my sorry ass with her to the nail salon?"

"Funny," Corey replied, furrowing his brows. "I was thinking that exact same thing."

The stranger followed with a chortle.

"That's a good question, my friend," the stranger said and looked closely into Corey's eyes. Then, after a close inspection, he shrugged. "I guess I just wanted to spend time with her."

"Nothing wrong with that," Corey said as he turned away.

"We've practically been strangers for the past month," he said as he carefully studied Corey's eyes again, both of them carefully watching Sally. "We hardly see each other. Lately, our schedules have been interfering with one another. I figured if this is the only time we could see each other, then why not tag along and be a good pet."

The stranger suddenly laughed, but Corey wasn't so quick to follow suit.

"The name's Corey, by the way," he said and then shook the stranger's hand.

"*Ben*," he said abruptly. "Ben Davis."

"So, what do you do for a living, Ben Davis?"

"Sales," he said. "Well, *vacuums*. I sell vacuums. It's not the most glamorous job in the world, but, you know how it goes, it pays the bills. Right?"

"Right," Corey said suspiciously.

"And occasionally pleases the wife with a mani-*whatever*."

Corey chortled, but it sounded forced and uncomfortable.

"Manicure."

"How about you?" Ben asked Corey. "What do you do for a J.O.B.?"

He said, "Occupational therapist."

Ben leaned back in amusement.

"Is that so?" Again, Ben looked closely at Corey's eyes, as if he was trying to read them. "Noble profession. Must be a very rewarding job, helping out people."

"I guess you can say that."

Ben's eyes moved down Corey's body and then finally rested on the bench beside him and then the paperback, *The Grapes of Wrath*, next to his hand.

Another nod.

"I take it you're a Steinbeck fan?"

"You're very observant."

"So, you're more of a lover of words," Ben said. "Not a Hemingway type of man."

"Well, I like them both," he said. "They both carry different styles of writing. One is more descriptive while the other not so descriptive. What it boils down to is how much time you have."

"*Always* not enough time."

Corey kept his eyes on Sally.

"Right," he said quietly.

Ben broke the silence with a laugh.

"I applaud you, man," he said jokingly.

"How so?"

"For your patience," Ben said as a grin crept onto his face. "I can't get through one freaking page of an owner's manual before my mind starts to wander into pussyland. The wife always talks about having one of them some day." Ben nodded at the children on the playground. His facial expression of near disgust. "Me, I don't have the time or the patience for them, you know, changing their diapers, always watching them. . . ."

"Well, it can be a full-time job," Corey replied, his voice now unsteady from the stranger's remarks. "Sally's not too bad."

". . . Reading them bedtime stories," he said over Corey. "I'd rather give them—I don't know—like an iTab and let it read to them. The way I look at it. In ten years or so, we'll have machines doing the dirty work for us."

Again, as Ben had been doing throughout the entire conversation, he kept looking closely at Corey's eyes, kept reading them.

Corey clenched his teeth from the stranger's remark.

"Well," he said patiently with a forged smile on his face, "I guess everybody is different."

"Right," Ben drawled and then checked his watch. "I better get going. Nice to meet you, Corey." He drew his attention to Corey's daughter, Sally, who, in return, directed her attention to the bench where her father was seated next to a stranger. For a second, her eyes flickered with a reflective iridescent light, which was identical to the tapetum lucidum found in the eyes of a cat. For a second, the blood rushed from the strange man's face, leaving it pale and ghostly. For a second, the man felt almost absent from his body as if he was sitting there but he *wasn't* there—not entirely. It was as if he misplaced his mind somewhere and now it was being held in a lost and found box. But it *only* lasted for a second. . .

Corey only caught a glimpse of the strange expression.

The stranger shook the numbness from his face, rotated and stretched his jaw, and vaguely said to Corey, "You have a. . . you have a special girl there."

"Thanks," Corey said strangely.

The stranger stood up, tipped his cap, and walked away.

Corey spun around, tempting to ask the stranger, Ben, what his interest was in Sally. *Or. . .* Corey thought as the question sat on the tip of his tongue, *was it just small talk?*

Either way, he was left in a weird state after the conversation with this man—the feeling one gets after being put on the spot in front of a large crowd of people.

After some thought, Corey ignored the question and drew his attention back to his daughter, who was staring at the stranger as he walked away.

—

THE strange man removed the ball cap from his head, revealing two plugs attached to each temple.

He got into the passenger seat of the black car.

In the driver seat sat Agent McClintock with that smug smile still on his face, however, less emphasized. The agent looked the same as before: same getup, same smug smile. The only difference in the agent's appearance was that this time he had a pink scar about the size of a close pin on the right side of his forehead from where his Pretty Miss Sunshine rammed his face into the wall.

"So. . . " he said, ". . . tell me, Ben Davis. How's the vacuum business?"

"It's called improvisation, smartass," the other agent said as he made himself comfortable in the passenger seat. He removed the circular sticky pads from each one of his temples, which were attached to a gray wire running through his curly hair, behind his head, and connected to a portable monitoring device on his belt.

Next, he removed the monitor from his belt and placed it on the dashboard. There was another monitor on the center console where Agent McClintock had been monitoring his partner's brain activity.

"It's not him," he said. "It's the kid."

"Well, Short," Agent McClintock said mockingly to his partner, "looks like your theory was right after all."

"Still four left," Agent Short said.

"Is it possible for it to skip a generation like that?"

"You know this business, McClintock," Agent Short said as he plugged that strange cubicle device into a laptop. "Anything is possible. . . "

—

IN the rear view mirror, Agent McClintock observed both Corey and his daughter strolling to their sedan, which was parked *precisely* three spaces behind them.

"Remember, McClintock, we're just after the kid," his partner said as he tightened a silencer over the end of the barrel. "I will handle the father. You get the kid. Any questions?"

—

As Corey secured Sally in the backseat, Agent Short, who was no longer wearing a baseball cap, approached Corey from behind.

"Excuse me," the agent said with his right hand held behind his back. "Corey, right?"

"Yes," Corey said warily as he leaned from the backseat of the car. Corey made eye contact with the strange man—this "Ben Davis" guy from the park—as well as the pale, vacant expression on his face. Then, he noticed how quickly he was approaching him. Corey turned to Sally. "Stay put," Corey said to her. He closed the door behind him and ambled closer to Agent Short. He asked, "Is everything okay?"

"My wife. . . " the agent said, his voice trembling, both eyes now widened, ". . . Have you seen my wife?"

"No," Corey said as the agent walked past him.

Agent Short stopped behind the sedan and looked around the street. His acting wasn't that good—amateur at best.

Corey studied him closely. His hand curled into a fist.

"It doesn't make any sense," Agent Short said, his breath labored, as Corey discreetly took a step closer to the driver's side door. "The girl who was doing her nails said she got up and ran out of the salon."

"That doesn't make any sense," Corey said as he kept his distance from Agent Short.

"You're telling me."

"Is there a number you can reach her at?"

"My battery's dead," he said, his breath now becoming more labored. "I meant to charge it this morning, but I had a lot on my mind. I must've forgotten." He turned to Corey, panic now in his eyes, "Can I use yours?"

"Uh. . . yeah. . . sure. . . " Corey pulled out a cell phone from his pocket. "Here you go."

"Thank you so much," Agent Short said with relief.

As he handed the phone to him, Agent Short pulled out a pistol from behind his back and shot Corey in the chest.

Corey stumbled backward—gasping for air—and then fell to the street where Agent Short shot him again, but this time directly between the eyes.

Once more, the agent looked around the street. The panic in his eyes was now gone. The agent didn't see anyone around—at least nobody that heard the two gunshots since they sounded no louder than a car horn that was tapped lightly, not fully honked. Then, Agent Short drew his eyes to the black car parked *precisely* three parking spots ahead where, at any second, Agent McClintock was supposed to be exiting.

Agent Short waited for a couple of seconds, but his partner—from where he could see—was sitting motion-lessly behind the steering wheel.

"Goddamn it," he seethed and checked on his partner.

When he arrived at the car, Agent McClintock was sit-ting in the driver's seat with his head flopped back against the headrest. A trail of blood was running from each one of his nostrils to the ridge of his chin. He pressed his fin-ger against the pulse along his partner's neck, but couldn't find a pulse. He rushed back to the sedan where he found Sally sitting quietly in the backseat.

Agent Short opened the back door.

Sally's face was long, her eyes glossy.

She asked the stranger, "What did you do to my fa-ther?"

The agent ignored the girl, turned his shoulder, and spotted a pedestrian who was chatting on his smartphone. The man was dressed in a cheap suit and staring directly at Agent Short. His face was long too like Sally's, as if he had been standing there the entire time.

"Shit," the agent said to himself. "Let's go," he said to Sally.

Sally asked, "Where's my father?"

"I'm afraid your father's not feeling well," the agent said and reached into the car. "He sai—"

He stopped halfway before he could wrap his hand around the girl.

As with the pedestrian chatting on the smartphone, his face was long. There was panic in his eyes, but this time it was real. No pretending. The sight of his face was like a man caught in the act—a long face, of course, eyes swol-len, something dumb inside them; it was as if he was about to steal a cub away from its mother, and its mother had unexpectedly paid the man a visit; and that bitch—oh that bitch—she wasn't a happy camper, and the man knew it too, knew that he didn't stand a chance from the icy expression on her face.

His dumb eyes were still focused on the woman stand-ing several feet outside the car, *not* Sally.

He tried to speak, but his jaw was locked in that silly opened position. His face turned from pale to a shade of gunmetal gray, but didn't completely turn to stone.

The other backseat door opened, revealing Chloe.

"Sally," Chloe said to the girl, "we have to go now."

"Where's my father?"

"He's gone," she said.

Chloe unbuckled Sally's seat belt and grabbed her hand.

"Do you trust me?" Chloe said, as she looked the girl in the eyes.

After a couple of tense seconds, Sally bobbed her head.

She wanted to hear a *yes* from the girl, but a bob of the head would have to make due for now. She helped Sally from the car.

"Cover your eyes, Sally," she said.

Sally did as the young woman demanded and covered her eyes with her left hand.

Chloe kneeled down and checked Corey's vitals with her free hand, but like Agent McClintock, he was dead.

As she rushed Sally to her car, a crowd had gathered around the pedestrian.

One man had turned into a dozen people, all scattered in a state of shock around him, smartphones attached to their ears; a couple of them took photos with their smart-phones while others filmed videos.

Two pedestrians—each one without a smartphone—broke away from the crowd and hurried toward Corey's sedan.

Before their faces could be identified, Chloe helped Sally into the backseat of a used gold-colored Nissan Maxima where Pegasus was sitting and drove off.

From the backseat, Sally asked Chloe, "Are you going to hurt me?"

"No, dear," she said as she glanced into the rear view mirror. "You're safe now."

"What do you want from me?"

She didn't answer Sally's question.

Instead, Chloe pulled out a CD from the center console and thought once or twice about playing it for Sally.

Sally asked, "Where are we going?"

"To Marseille," she said. "Marseille, France."

"Why?"

"Because we have to," Chloe said sternly. "That's why."

Chloe passed two cruisers—with their sirens blaring—as she turned onto another street.

She checked the rear view mirror and carefully followed the cruisers with her eyes. The cruisers kept driving. In the back of her mind, she knew there would be more of them.

ATLANTA, GEORGIA
APRIL 30, 2015

INSIDE a little pitiless place called the television world where things appeared larger than what they seemed in reality, she was the white pointer in a tank full of blood-thirsty piranhas. They all wanted a piece of her, just a nibble of the elusive great white, but they knew they could *not* touch her, *not* even in a world of lies and deception, for this was her world and she was the shark and nobody fucked with the shark.

In the television world, her name was Bobbie Chase, *the* Bobbie Chase, aka "The Shark," but in real life, her name was Barbara Summerset, a valedictorian from the class of '75—needless to say, an intelligent lady. Those who didn't personally know Ms. Summerset knew her as Bobbie Chase, the volatile, quick-drawing, bitch-slapping host of the hot TV show, *On the Case w/ Ms. Bobbie Chase* or one of the *New York Times* "Top Ten Best-Selling Authors of 2014," most notably recognized for her highly acclaimed mystery series called the *Erin Jaden Files*—similar to the Nancy Drew stuff, only less adolescent, more adult in nature, and riddled with hackneyed aphorisms and worn out themes and lame, two-dimensional characters who lacked all common sense (and most of

those characters in her books, mainly the villains, were
based on suspects whom Bobbie had profiled on her show);
however, tweaked for the market. Bobbie Chase was a
woman whom people loved to hate. And that hate gave
Bobbie power. However, one would possibly ask how Barbara Summerset went from the top of her class to a ven-
omous TV host. It happened a month into her sophomore
year at West Madison. It was actually her roommate,
Connie, who forced Barbara to come out. There was a
party at Beta's house, and the dean's nephew, the star
quarterback of the football team, was going to be there.
His name was Allen R. Cornwall, and he was the kind of
guy who, as a youngster, enjoyed stepping on flowers for
the hell of it, not because of the way flowers smelled or
looked, but because of the way they made people feel good
inside. She had a crush on Allen (every time Barbara
passed him in the courtyard, she would get all queasy, and
the *one* time Allen had spoken to her was when he asked
her for a pen to write down another chick's number; she
didn't say much to Allen during the brief exchange, and if
she did, she couldn't remember a damn thing—something
like "Bye, Allen. I mean. . . hi, Allen. My. . . my name is
Allen. No. Your name is Allen. Duh! I mean. . . Barbara.
My name is Barbara *or* Barb, like the doll you play with,
not you, of course, I wasn't implying that you played with
dolls. . . I mean, me, I used to play with them, Barbie
dolls, but only spelled without the *i* and the *e*."). Allen
looked at Barbara the same way Allen did with every girl
on campus, as another piece of ass. Little did Barbara
know what she was getting into when she crossed paths
with Allen after he did a keg stand and accidentally
knocked over her beer. Allen was hammered. Barbara
wasn't—not yet. Allen fetched Barbara a new beer. Then,
one drink led to two drinks. Then, three. While she was
working her way through the fourth drink, he invited her
upstairs where they could get to know each other a little
better. Barbara entered what alcoholics call the "blackout
stage" after she finished the fourth beer. Next thing Barbara knew, she was lying in a strange bed, Allen's finely

sculpted body straddled over hers. By the time she came to her senses, she realized exactly what Allen was doing to her. She sobered up and tried to push him off. Allen refused. Allen kept pursuing. Barbara resisted. Allen was *still* drunk, but Barbara wasn't; and she remembered every last detail of what went down at that party, the horror of the pain and the pleasure—but the pain came out as the victor and the pleasure, Barbara's own tag line to remind her how low a man could go. She barely made it to the campus police the next morning. She was mortified after what happened to her. What young woman wouldn't be? Someone needed to know what he had done to her. Walking was a task all by itself. Each step was a reminder of what he had done to her. And Barbara had the cuts to show on her arms and legs, the bruises on her face and genitals.

In Allen's defense, he had scratch marks on his back; however, he couldn't remember how they got there.

As soon as Barbara mentioned who had done this to her, that "arrogant piece of dog shit, Allen, yeah, that's right, Allen Cornwall," Barbara's case never saw the light of day.

As far as Barbara knew, it was swept under the rug, never to be brought up ever again.

Barbara never let what happened at West Madison get the best of her.

Instead, she used it as a weapon.

And she thrived off it too as it came from all angles, especially the hate: the trolls on the Internet, journalists, and then the piranhas whom she'd argue with until she was blue in the face—even the bottom feeders too. Snarky lawyers were the tastiest of all the guests she had on her TV show, for she was the shark and what better treat for a shark than a snarky analytical lawyer; and she ate up those sneaky insects too like a ravenous creature with an unlimited appetite.

There was even a drinking game named after Bobbie. The college kids called it Bobbiehead. The instructions consisted of two rules. The first rule: each participant must take of sip of his or her drink every time Bobbie mentioned the words *I* or *me* or *my* (for an example: *I* this—drink—*I* that—drink—*me, me, me, my, my, my*—drink to the sixth power; and if she used a combination of words, the participant had to chug his or her drink). Second rule: participants must punch a hole in the wall if Bobbie mentioned the word *justice*. Most people didn't make it till the end of the show before passing out or breaking his or her knuckles or worse, getting punched in the face.

The game wasn't for the faint of heart.

Outside the television world, however, Bobbie was an ordinary woman who lived a small life in a small town outside Atlanta. She paid the rent like everybody else. Shopped for groceries like everybody else. Changed the oil like everybody else. Watched reruns of her show every night like everybody else.

When Bobbie left work, she was no longer Bobbie Chase.

Her name was Barbara Summerset, and she was just another fish in the sea.

—

JUST two days prior to what happened in Seattle, there was a string of murders: a father of two boys; a college student who was studying to be a physicist; and lastly, a divorcée in charge of running a multi-million dollar advertisement agency, which left both Chloe and Sally grounded. After a speedy investigation, all three of the murders were pinned to Chloe (the Feds even had the video footage, as well as a witness to her killing two of the victims). It was all the Company's doing, though. The footage was altered. The person responsible for committing these violent acts was an imposter made to appear as if Chloe was on the scene of the crime when, in fact, Chloe was *not*. They figured if they couldn't catch her, then maybe the cops could.

And that was when the shark came into the picture.

Just two weeks after the three murders, Bobbie ran a special coverage dedicated to Chloe called *Catching A Cold-Blooded Killer.* No other network covered Chloe like Bobbie, and it had certainly become evident to most in the media, as well as viewers, that Chloe had turned into a borderline obsession for Bobbie—her own perfect little project. Even the people in charge of the network, YN, short for YOUR NETWORK, said it was damn good television.

For Chloe, killing Bobbie was going to be hard because, with all of the false accusations aside, she admired Ms. Chase's passion. Like Chloe, Bobbie too was a woman seeking truth and justice for the person who did her wrong and she used her show as a platform to catch the bad guys. However, over several years on television, Bobbie had become blind to the truth, a woman stuck on her own self, trying to save *you* and tell *your* story when, in fact, *she* was the one who needed the saving.

—

BOBBIE met her demise on a Thursday, the Thirtieth of April, a few weeks after the video of Chloe rescuing Sally went viral. As long as Bobbie was *still* on the air, Chloe knew that her life and Sally's life would remain in great jeopardy. What Chloe thought would be extinguishing a fire was actually throwing gasoline on it, resulting in one helluva mess; and making an example of this erratic TV host, who got paid millions for making examples of other people—guilty or not—was exactly what Chloe thought needed to be done.

—

PEOPLE were calling it the selfie seen around the world.

Nobody knew who was behind it all, who turned the television host/best-seller author, Bobbie "The Shark" Chase, into a courtyard statue.

Except for the Company. They knew.

———

WHILE Sally was waiting in the car, Chloe snuck her way into YN main studio headquarters without a problem.

She had one scale left in the tin can of Zigzags, which wasn't even a full scale at all but the shavings of half of one. She downed it with one swallow, but it wasn't quite enough. She needed a little extra boost. So, she used a razor and scraped the residue of the scale from the can and snorted a line of it and then rubbed the last remaining dust over the top of her gums.

That did the trick.

Next, she found the surveillance room, gazed the first security guard, and directed him to stop *all* recording of surveillance videos.

He did.

No problem.

The second guard wasn't a breeze like the first one.

She didn't kill him, though.

Wasn't her style.

Instead, Chloe left him with a fractured arm and a couple of broken ribs.

But he'd live.

She made it to Studio D without getting spotted by any other personnel.

The red ON AIR sign above the door was lit.

Bobbie was at the end of her opening monologue, which consisted of her jabbering about Chloe Dorsey—nothing new—and how much of a threat she was to the American people and how, if she wasn't captured by the authorities as soon as possible, then *nobody* was safe ("That's right!" she seethed on the air. "Lock your doors, people! Hide the children! Be afraid! Be *very* afraid! As long as this monster remains on our streets, nobody is safe! I mean nobody!"), when her eyes crossed the TelePrompTer and mistakenly found their way into Chloe's bright eyes underneath a solid black cap that she stole from a guard. Bobbie's thin, dark eyes widened first and then her mouth stretched outward like a yawn—her face now left in a gape. A shade of paleness washed over her stupid face followed by an involuntary sting from where the blood raced through her veins and constricted as the blood hardened. The strange sensation felt as if a thousand hands were giving her Indian rug burns over her entire body. And that was when it happened, the *im*possible, the host of the show, *On the Case w/ Ms. Bobbie Chase*, as well as the New York Times best-selling author, was given a dramatic makeover from head to toe on national television. Bobbie Chase, the mystery author who devoted her career exploiting other people, only to make a quick buck, the author who was best known for her shocking and yet paradoxical endings, the author who coined the phrase, "Tell it to the Judge, Loser!" received the ultimate surprise of a lifetime.

So, naturally, Chloe had a zinger of her own: "Put that in the fucking book."

Immediately after it happened, and everybody inside Studio D, including producers and cameramen alike, were left as dumbfounded as Bobbie herself, an unruly intern named Abe ran up behind Bobbie's stone body and took a selfie with her.

Following the selfie, Abe posted the photo on his My-Circle page. #WTF!!! #OMG #HolyShit #ROMFAL #HAHA #NoMoreCoffee4U #Go2HellBeeeahch ♥ ☺

—

IN just two days, the selfie went viral.

Any individual who was connected to the Internet or owned a television or read a newspaper knew Chloe's face.

Unless they lived under a rock, they *knew* her face.

Perhaps too well.

So, Chloe had no other choice than to leave the country.

She ended up dropping off Pegasus at a local dog park where there were lots of other dogs frolicking or whatever dogs did at a dog park. She was disheartened to say goodbye to the dog, but it had to be done.

Since Chloe had to use the gaze on nearly every single person who looked twice at her, including police officers,

Chloe didn't know how much longer she could use the gaze to its fullest potential. The more people she came across, the lesser its strength.

Ever since Chloe left Whisperfront, the time spent buying an airplane ticket for herself and Sally (Chloe didn't actually purchase the tickets; Chloe gazed the perky ticketing agent and told her to give her two tickets to Paris), as well as making her way through airport security, was the most Chloe had used the gaze. There were many side effects—as presumed—but the fever was child's play compared to using the gaze to such an extent. Her physical appearance had worsened. Her face was colorless; she had dark bags underneath her eyes, which were bloodshot. One of the main side effects was Chloe's loss of weight, and she lost plenty. She looked like a junkie who was itching for a quick fix. However, no matter how sick Chloe was, she had to stay on her toes with every blink of an eye. One missed person meant one potential witness. And one potential witness meant the Company was right on their tails. Chloe had little time to eat; and when Chloe did, she could hardly hold down any food. She had little to no energy too. She kept herself hydrated with plenty of fluids. Crowds were the worst and most debilitating. Walking through a crowd was no different than running three miles without any break. She ended using the same disguise for herself and Sally—their outward appearance varying solely on her current state. So, when people crossed their paths, all they saw were past reflections of somebody they saw moments ago. This particular skill was known as "accessing," and it was one of the key components to her gaze. Her father was well skilled when it came to accessing—hence why he was one of the best negotiators in the city of Lansford. Nearly zero crime rate during his service. This particular skill had taken many weeks of practice for her to fully acquire. Chloe compared it to "déjà vu," only it was slightly different than most people's interpretations. It wasn't like flipping on a light switch. More like rewiring the circuit. The technique was similar to highlighting a word in a document, deleting that word, and then copying another word and pasting that word in the old word's place. Instead of words, Chloe used the person's thoughts—recent images, mainly—and then she'd reroute them through certain parts of the brain, starting from the visual cortex located in the occipital lobe and then channel through various pathways, or "streams," in the brain, such as the ventral and the dorsal stream—most of the images came from the temporal lobe, which dealt with visual memories, *new* images, *faces*. She'd highlight an image from a person's temporal lobe, copy, and then paste that image in the occipital lobe. It was like playing a game of *Pong*, streaming from one lobe to the other, and then going back and forth, back and forth, back and forth, replacing images in her and Sally's place (imagine doing that for hundreds of people. It was taxing to say the least.). She did this for *every* single person in the airport. She'd highlight an image—for instance—of an elderly woman or a janitor or whoever that individual saw just minutes ago or, hell, even an hour or two ago (maybe this person had a particular liking for that person), copy that image, and then paste it inside the person's mind.

And when that person looked at Chloe and Sally, they experienced something they could not explain.

Déjà vu.

That's what Chloe called it.

They made it past customs by the skin of their teeth without a passport, only two travel brochures of the Rocky Mountains that Chloe grabbed from a newsstand.

The great thing about the gaze was that they didn't need a passport, just something similar.

The gaze would handle it, no sweat.

A surveillance video captured the two with *no* disguise—no passport either, only brochures—which the Company would use to its advantage.

They took a direct flight from Hartsfield-Jackson to Charles de Gaulle.

PARIS, FRANCE
MAY 4, 2015

ONCE they arrived in Paris, they kept their heads down for a few days.

Chloe and Sally didn't have time to sightsee or enjoy the city of lights.

These amenities were no longer a part of Chloe or Sally's life.

They stayed in a hostel on the edge of Paris called Le Village, which was known as the Biltmore of hostels across all of Europe but was more like a smelly rat's nest.

For Chloe, it was perfect, *ideal*.

For Sally, not so much.

However, most of the hostel's traffic came from students and backpackers, and Chloe was the least of their worries.

They stayed in Le Rat's Nest until they were fit enough to take a train to Marseille.

During the downtime, Chloe spent most of her time resting and recovering. Sally rested a little bit too, although she spent a lot of her time practicing the gaze on cockroaches and earwigs and rats. Chloe was amazed by the young girl's skill level. Insects and animals were easy for Sally—second nature. Humans were the trickiest. Sally wasn't as strong as Chloe when it came to using the gaze; although, in time, she would get better.

MARSEILLE, FRANCE
MAY 8, 2015

THERE was a loud and hollow *thud* outside Juliet's room, as well as a *clank* from where Chloe had rammed the orderly's head into a metal pipe.

Moments later, the door swung open, only to reveal the mysterious person standing at the doorway—fists bloody and all.

Juliet was strapped to the bed, motionless. All four restraints were fastened extra tight over both wrists, as well

72

as her ankles, after the botched suicide attempt yesterday during her mother's visit.

"Hello, Juliet," Chloe said from the doorway.

Juliet didn't budge from the voice, not an inch. The air, Juliet sniffed, was different from the others.

Pas la mère (Not mother), she thought, or the doctors.

With her head in the same still position, she moved her eyes to the right.

In the corner of her eye, she found a strange woman standing at the doorway, the mystery person—tall, Juliet saw, attractive, familiar.

Approaching Juliet, Chloe said, "I've come a long way to find you."

As she stood over Juliet, they made eye contact.

Something happened to both Chloe and Juliet, something that they couldn't explain.

– 1 1 . 1 6 . 2 0 4 8 –

MARK said to Chloe, "On your father's last audio recording, he referred to this particular surge of energy as 'the link.' Is there any information you can share with us to help us further understand this 'link?'"

Chloe said, "No."

"Think about your son, Chloe."

"Before I had a chance to understand the link, you people destroyed it."

"Not us, Chloe," Mark said. "You. *You* destroyed it."

"He was one of yours, not mine."

"Used to be one of ours."

Chloe sighed.

"Same fucking thing."

MARSEILLE, FRANCE
MAY 9, 2015

THE next day, the two agents sent by the Company arrived at Clinique Saint Marc.

Juliet Baudin was no longer a patient, said one of the doctors.

When they asked the doctors about Juliet's whereabouts or where she might've been taken, the doctors said that Juliet was transferred to a mental hospital in America.

"Death Valley," the doctor said.

They asked the doctors if this was some kind of joke.

The doctors at Clinique Saint Marc didn't get the joke.

The agents did.

And now, it was on. . .

– 1 1 . 1 6 . 2 0 4 8 –

CHLOE couldn't stand the smell of the white room, the sterile atmosphere. It was like being stuck inside a doctor's office. The only thing keeping her mind off the awful smell was him—Mark.

She didn't exactly know who or what Mark was, but she did know that he wasn't a *he*, and yet he looked everything like a *he* from the suit he wore to the way he spoke—the smooth southern drawl of Fort Worth, Texas, underneath the rich and resonant cut of Brooklyn, New York. It was North versus South in one voice. Like bleach and vinegar, they never quite mix well. The people responsible for Mark thought it would make Mark seem more distinct—*unique*—and, for a buyer's market, more sellable. The first time Chloe met him in a mandatory introduction, she became overly suspicious of what Mark was when she smelled his inner makings underneath a heavy layer of off-brand cologne. When she lost the right side of her hearing in Helena, Montana, after a violent car wreck, her other senses were enhanced—especially her sense of smell. Chloe could even smell a sickness inside a person's body. And the employees of JeneCorp reeked of it. However, when Chloe smelled Mark, she smelled nothing, except for the sour cologne that he was wearing. Then, when Chloe gazed Mark, she saw nothing inside him. He had no memories or childhood, only a void of darkness.

After Chloe was given an hour for a break, which consisted of a meal and a book—the meal: a bowl of pureed-whatever to not only hydrate, but also to restore balance to her body after a cup of coffee (she called it a bowl of crap because that was what she thought it tasted like; the employees called the stuff *feed*, which had the consistency of jello, but it was slightly tepid and lumpy); and then the book: a wrinkled paperback of *Around the World in Eighty Days* by Jules Verne—two guards escorted Chloe to the aluminum table.

Times had changed.

Over time, things got much smaller and sleeker, including the visors, which had been reduced down to a pair of contact lenses. It was fairly easy to spot the new upgrades. The eyes looked the same; however, they had a particular look about them, as if they had been dipped in milk and left to settle.

The two guards sat Chloe down across from Mark, who was seated upright with an eClipse tablet in front of him.

Chloe looked much older than her age—an added ten plus years from all of the running and gunning. She had very little color in her face. She had dark rings around her eyes and two red dots underneath each eyelid, which looked like the marks of a vampire from where they had prodded her with needles and extracted tears from her eyes. Her hair was thin and wrapped in a ponytail. And she was starting to show more gray, too, which she kind of liked—Chloe thought it made her look important, as if she had been around the block once or twice.

Mark first asked, "How was your lunch, Chloe?"

"Just wonderful," she said.

"You don't like the feed either?"

"Well, looks like we have something in common after all."

"It would appear so."

"Let's get this over with. . . "

"Very well," Mark said to Chloe. "Please start where you left off last time, in Marseille."

"Sure," she said. "When we left Marseille, that's when all the pieces of the puzzle started to come together."

Mark scrolled through the notes on the table. "You said you got sick before you arrived in Paris," Mark said, reading the digital notes. "So, why didn't you become stronger when you joined forces with Sally?"

"Too young, still growing," Chloe answered. "The gaze came natural to her, but she wasn't as powerful as Juliet. When I met up with Juliet and looked into her eyes for the first time. . . the power I felt, it was unlike any power I'd ever felt before."

"Was it the same with the other two?"

"Vivian, yes, although it took a little more convincing."

"And how about Ms. Ganguly?"

"No."

"Tell me about Ms. Lerwick. . . Vivian," Mark suddenly corrected. "What was it like when you first met Vivian?"

"When I met Vivian," Chloe said after a long pause, "I saw a woman who was once like me—on the outside, that is. She was a person lost in a strange world, like a stranger in a strange land. The gaze never worked on her. Even. . . even if I tried to see what Vivian was thinking, all I got was someone else's thoughts, not hers."

"How about Gabby Reynolds?"

"But you already know what happened to her."

"If she was alive," Mark said to Chloe, "what do you think the gaze would've been like on her?"

CANTERBURY, ENGLAND
MAY 12, 2015

THE third "other" was Gabby Reynolds, and she was already dead.

Five days ago, her body was found along an underground pipe of River Westbourne, closest to Sloane Square, which was also known as one of the many "lost" rivers in London, by a group of young skaters. Gabby had been dead for over twenty-four hours, and the pungent smell emitting from the body suggested that it was getting pretty ripe. Her murderer had slit her throat, and then removed both of her eyes, as well as her tongue, postmortem.

Three days ago, after a thorough examination, Gabby was laid to rest in Charlemagne Falls Cemetery.

Chloe and the gang visited Gabby's legal guardian, Charlotte, at her quaint townhouse in Canterbury where the three learned about Gabby's death and how she had been murdered just five days prior to their visit and that her killer was *still* at large. In order to protect not only her own identity, but also Sally and Juliet's identity as well, Chloe never told Charlotte they were all related to Gabby through a mutual father. Instead, Chloe told Charlotte that she was a friend of Gabby's and that she hadn't seen Gabby since she left for Kingston University—an art major, Gabby was. Chloe remembered, word for word, what her father said on the disc he had left for her (the information obtained by none other than Diego): *Her name is Gabby Reynolds, an art major. She aspires to one day work at the Natural History Museum in London, England. She attends Kingston University. When Gabby's not in school, she resides in Canterbury, England, with a woman who goes by the name of Charlotte Reynolds, her adopted mother.* She bought the story (for now, at least) and decided to welcome Chloe and the others into her home. They drank warm tea and looked at photographs that she had kept of Gabby from adolescence to young adulthood. Chloe came across a photograph of another girl named Vivian, who—Chloe would later learn—was Gabby's biological sister. Gabby wasn't the *only* sibling, Chloe realized. She had a twin sister who was separated from Gabby at birth. When they came across the newspaper article about the kidnapping, Charlotte told them the story: There was a woman named Maggie Philips, a nurse who worked at the same hospital where Gabby's biological mother, Elizabeth Holmes, or "Liz" was what they called her, gave birth. Ms. Philips kidnapped the twins and sold them to two wealthy families—Gabby went to a wealthy couple in Bristol, and Vivian to a couple in Liverpool. Months later, after the search for baby Gabby and baby Vivian went cold, Liz's sister, Bryony, who had been staying with Liz after the kidnapping, went to check on her sister's well-being, only to find her dead body dangling from a noose in the closet, as well as a note in her pocket, telling Bryony that she was sorry and that she could no longer live with the guilt of losing her two babies. Two years later, an industrialist from Bristol walked in on his wife having an affair with another man. He killed his wife and then her lover, and then killed himself—what the bobbies called a "good ole fashion murder-suicide." Little Gabby saw it all, each and every murder. Remarkably, Gabby was never affected by what happened in Bristol. Gabby remembered breaking her wrist while swinging from the mushroom tree when she was six years old. She remembered the time she received over a dozen stitches while playing the game cricket with a silly two by four and a rock for the first time—Jeremiah, "Buck Teeth," accidentally smacking her in the face with the two by four. She remembered chipping her tooth when she was the age of eleven. But she *never* remembered what happened in Bristol. Gabby was shuffled through three orphanages until Bryony finally found her in Southampton. Her aunt raised her in an open home. *Never* smothered her. *Never* neglected Gabby either. She gave her love and attention and spoiled her whenever she needed it. She lived with Bryony for four years—making her eight—until she passed from surgical complications. Gabby was placed in another orphanage for a little over a year until a younger couple (who, like her first parents in Bristol, couldn't have children) adopted her. And that was when Charlotte entered the picture. She and her lifelong partner, Addison, whom she called *Big Addie*, which, when she said it, sounded like Big Daddy, brought her back to Reading where they raised Gabby until she left for college.

Just a year after Gabby left, Big Addie died from a massive stroke, and Charlotte decided to move back to her hometown in Canterbury to take care of her ailing mother.

—

Liz, Gabby's biological mother, had met Leon on the cusp of stardom. Liz was there at the beginning when Leon became the great Freeze of Lansford. They were off and on, Chloe learned from a couple of articles that Charlotte kept through her many years of research—after Big Addie passed, she dedicated a lot of her time digging up dirt on Gabby and her background, not because she wanted to expose her or anything malicious like that, but because, if Gabby was ever curious to know who her mother was or where she came from, then she had the proof to show her. There were a couple of pictures of Leon and Liz, one taken when they were leaving a nightclub in uptown Lansford. Liz had wavy brunette hair, glowing skin, nice features. She disappeared from the scene for a couple of years, stumbled into a bad coke problem, went to rehab, got her act together, and then, later, at the height of Leon's fame, they rekindled a flame. But the flame didn't last too long; in fact, it burned out as soon as it got too hot. Liz got knocked up, flew back to England with—little did she know—two buns in the oven.

Six months later, after Liz brought the news to Leon, she received a fat check in the mail.

Money had a peculiar way of keeping mouths shut and secrets hidden.

However, there was one thing money couldn't buy. . .

— 1 1 . 1 6 . 2 0 4 8 —

CHLOE slowly raised her head from the table and said to Mark in a trance-like state, "The chase began when we were visiting the cemetery where Gabby was laid to rest. Even though we had never met her, she was a part of us. Paying our respects was *the least* we could do."

(*Chloe placed a set of blue roses on top of the head-stone.*)

"As we were about to leave," Chloe said, "I heard a sound over my shoulder. I turned to Juliet and she was holding her side—I saw the pain in her face. She removed her hand from her side. That was when I saw the blood."

(*In a state of shock, Juliet removed her bloody hand from her left side.*)

"The bullet went in and out," Chloe said. "If it were three inches to the right, she would've been dead. Then, I heard more of those same sounds; pieces of headstone shot up at us. One piece caught Sally in the face, nearly blinding her."

(*Chloe honed the gaze and found the sniper camped behind a bush.*)

"I knew the whole thing was a setup," Chloe said to Mark, "the whole visit. . . they were watching us the entire time."

(*There were a couple of men with assault rifles. They moved as if they were trained properly, as if they were trained not to feel anything at all. The sniper, Chloe saw, was dressed differently from the other men. He didn't appear as if he was working with the Company; in fact, none of them did.*

But maybe they were.

She didn't know.)

Mark asked, "Was Charlotte aware?"

"I don't know," she said. "Later, I found out Charlotte and her mother were murdered. Both of them were gunned down. Whoever killed Gabby was trying to kill us."

"Who did you think was behind it all?"

Chloe said, "Whoever they were, they were good. . ."

HONG KONG, CHINA
MAY 19, 2015

WITH enough money one could buy anything in the world, well, *mostly* anything.

Thomas S. Lerwick, CEO of the multinational oil and gas corporation, Swick Petroleum, bought a daughter, dropped the name Vivian, and named her after his mother, Gwendolyn Lerwick.

At the age of seven, young Gwendolyn was diagnosed with having Aniridia in both eyes—a disorder involving the absence of an iris.

A year later, Gwendolyn decided to snip off the *dolyn* from Gwendolyn and simply go by the name Gwen, since the name Gwendolyn sounded too witchy.

At the age of eleven, Gwen developed a particular curiosity in electronics, mainly computer software and hardware. Her father bought Gwen a PC for her twelfth birthday. For the next three years, she learned the ins and outs of a computer, literally. She had a thing for taking apart computers and then putting them back together. She liked to tweak them and make them better, a trade she picked up from her father.

At the age of fourteen—going on fifteen—her father asked her to pick any place in the world to visit and whatever Gwen picked, he'd take her there for a week, no more, no less.

For her fifteenth birthday, Gwen spent a week in Hong Kong with her father. Best birthday present ever.

When they came back to Liverpool, Gwen couldn't wait to go back to Hong Kong.

At the age of sixteen, she graduated from secondary school and spent the entire summer at an internship program at Linal Technologies, founded by Lin Chu and Lan Hsiung—all of it organized by her father, of course.

At the age of nineteen, Gwen Lerwick was working at Linal Technologies as a software programmer.

Nine years later, she was visited by a woman who went by the name Chloe Dorsey.

She found her on an unseasonably muggy Tuesday night.

It started when their eyes crossed paths. Gwen was seated at one end of the subway car, Chloe Dorsey at the opposite end. They were unlike anything Gwen had ever seen before—her eyes like two iridescent pearls resting inside black clamshells. This was another talent the gaze had offered. Chloe had picked up the talent on her own while spending time with the others in her bloodline. Anyone who possessed the gaze could spot his or her own kind. This, of course, was new to Chloe. Her father had never mentioned anything about the light. It had become clear to Chloe after she found Juliet. Those in the bloodline carried a special light in their eyes—like a cat's eyes in the dark, glowing when seen at certain angles; however, this light could never been seen by any other man or woman who did *not* possess the gaze, only people who possessed the gaze/or were being gazed.

Gwen had only seen this peculiar pair of eyes once in her brief existence, and that was when she was just a baby.

(*Two strange lights*, Gwen remembered, flickering like a dying flame—the image was like two candlelit windows in a cottage sitting on the rolling hills of North Canterbury, a place that Gwen would never come to know, never come to love, no detail of the cottage, only an outline of its handmade foundation and its two burning windows—two *tiny* strange lights being taking away by the arms of a nurse, she remembered, the nurse shushing and then concealing that light with a gray shawl).

The light.

She had never seen that light again until now. . .

She was an American too from what Gwen gathered, *not* Chinese, and the jeans that she wore were dark and tight, as if they had been airbrushed over her legs with fine craftsmanship; and they matched the black leather jacket and holey white tee that she wore underneath.

As the subway car proceeded forward through the tunnel, this woman, Gwen saw through the corner of her eye, moved with the shadows until she arrived at a standing post not too far from where Gwen was seated.

Each flash and flicker of the shoddy light above brought out the woman's narrow eyes, the two tiny globes of iridescent light aimed directly at Gwen.

Something in her eyes, she noticed, something strange about her appearance.

Before Gwen had a chance to see the woman in her entirety, Chloe vanished back into the shadows.

—

WHEN the subway car stopped at its destination, Gwen thought she saw those same two eyes exiting through a crowd of people.

Hesitant at first, Gwen eventually exited the car as well.

She searched through the crowd, trying not to make it too obvious, and occasionally peeked over her shoulder.

Those two eyes were nowhere to be found.

—

WHEN Gwen left the subway, the eyes were back, and they were following her.

She walked two blocks along the sidewalk, making sure to stay close to other people until she made it back home.

—

"GOOD evening, Ms. Lerwick," the doorman greeted Chloe at the main entrance of her building.

"Good evening," Chloe replied, her sharp eyes cutting right through the doorman's slanted eyes.

The doorman didn't say a word after the brief encounter with Chloe, only the first draft of a word, which sounded something like *huh*.

In a state of perplexity, he watched Chloe walk away.

She approached the front counter where a security guard was reading a manga comic book.

The guard placed the book aside and asked Chloe, "How can I help you this evening?"

———

PASSING her building until she lost the strange woman with the strange eyes, Gwen walked another block before she decided to return home, which was at a luxurious high-rise apartment on Queen's Road Central.

She stopped at the main entrance before entering.

Next to the door was a man standing there in a daze. His name was Chu, the doorman.

"Are you all right, Chu?" Gwen asked the doorman.

He raised his head and looked into Gwen's eyes, as if she was a stranger. His previous perplexity was gone, and now Chu was standing there like a toddler who didn't quite understand words. Chu could hear them, the words, and absorb them like a sponge; however, he didn't know the full meaning of them. Gwen said Chu's name again.

As before, Chu replied with a disjointed *huh.*

"Are you all right?" Gwen asked again.

Chu furrowed his brows and wandered down the sidewalk.

———

"BACK so soon," the security guard said in Chinese.

"Back?" Gwen said. "I never left."

The guard laughed, merrily at first, and then it died with the clearing of his throat.

"Did you forget something?"

Gwen said seriously, "Excuse me. . . "

"The card I gave you," he said, "did it work?"

"What card?"

More perplexity.

"The card I just gave you."

"I'm sorry."

The expression on the security guard's face emptied.

"*The card. . .* "

Gwen didn't have a response.

"Remember?"

"Yes," Gwen said. "Sorry."

—

THE entire ride on the elevator was a blur to Gwen.

Has my Chinese gotten that bad?

Gwen wondered if the important things like speech and hearing were starting to fade, and all of these things were now being replaced with ones and zeroes, binary code. After all, she spent more time staring into the dead eyes of a machine than an actual person. If one stared for too long into the machine, would one eventually become a part of the machine?

This wasn't the first time she had thought about these theories. Her immediate response was always the same.

But that would be ridiculous, she thought.

The sudden *ding* of the elevator pulled Gwen from her racing thoughts. She exited the elevator and walked to her apartment. The smell in the hallway was familiar—a little sweet and a little sour, sweet enough to attract and yet sour enough to repel. She didn't think too much about it, the smell.

When she arrived at her apartment, she slid the key card into the lock and opened the door, only to find that strange smell from the hallway.

She entered the dark apartment and placed her bag on the kitchen table.

Just as Gwen switched on the lights along the kitchen wall, a woman's voice—Chloe's voice—said from a glass desk in front of the window, "Nice place you got here. . . "

She had no other response than a loud gasp. She tracked the voice to the dark silhouette seated behind her desk. The colorful lights from the brilliant skyline outside the window lit one side of Chloe's pallid face. She was also carrying that same light in her eyes from the subway, Gwen noticed.

"What. . . what. . . are you doing in my apart. . . "

Her body fell into a state of shock. The muscles in her throat and chest tightened, causing it harder to breath.

"Relax, Ms. Lerwick," Chloe said, as Gwen took a step away from the intruder. "I'm not going to hurt you."

Her breath became labored, body staggered.

She uttered, "You. . . you've been following me."

"Yes," Chloe said as she leaned forward into the pale light. "I have."

Gwen said suddenly, "Wa. . . hat do you want? Money?"

"I don't want your money."

"Then *what* do you want?"

"I just want to talk."

"Who are you?"

"I don't have time to explain who I am," Chloe said as Gwen bravely took a step forward. That was when Chloe gazed her, Gwen. A staticky feeling suddenly ran across the top of Chloe's skin, causing the hair to erect. She was different, Chloe realized, not like Sally or Juliet. When she gazed Gwen, she felt weaker, not stronger. Chloe felt corrupted. *She was much. . .* different. Chloe remained poised and said to Gwen, "Your life is in grave danger, Gwen."

"How do you know my name?" she asked and took yet another step forward.

This time she found Chloe's eyes and looked into them, that strange light, the light of a cat's eye.

Chloe said carefully to Gwen, "I know everything about you, Gwen Lerwick. Gwen Lerwick isn't even your real name. It's Vivian Holmes, and you're the daughter of Elizabeth Holmes, your real mother."

As before, Gwen had nothing to say in return.

"If you don't come with me tonight," she said, "they will kill you."

"Who?" Gwen cried. "What are you talking about?"

"At any moment," she said, "a group of highly-trained assassins can storm through that door behind you and kill us both."

"I'm calling the police," she said as she made an attempt toward the smartphone in her bag.

"I wouldn't do that if I were you."

"Watch me, you crazy bitch. . ."

Gwen grabbed the smartphone from her bag.

"You think I don't know what you're going through. . ."

She only got through a digit before she suddenly paused.

"It took a lot of courage to do what you did last night."

"What?"

"You know what I'm talking about."

Gwen shook her head.

"No," she said angrily. "I don't."

"I was once like you, Vivian. . . ."

"My name's Gwen—"

". . . You can't quite put a name to it, that feeling," she said over Gwen. "But it's always there, when you wake up, when you go to work, when you come home at night. I used to have the same feeling. Still do, at times. Eventually, I've learned to live with it." She stood up from the chair, which caused Gwen to flinch. Now, Gwen took a step back, gradually. "You know what I'm talking about, the emptiness."

Gwen tried to speak, but her lips quivered.

"You could've taken the easy way out," she said as she inched closer to Gwen, "like you almost did last night, but you know in the back of your mind that maybe it will be there. . . even after death."

Gwen said, "You've been watching me?"

(*She stepped outside her body and saw herself standing on the ledge of the high-rise apartment building. Tonight was the night, she had told herself on the subway home from work. Tonight was the night I would finally receive the smooch of death.*

She took one step before retracting her foot back onto the ledge. She got off the ledge and ran back inside and locked the sliding door behind her.)

"No," Chloe said. "All I have to do is look into your eyes and know that last night was *not* your night to die. *You*, Vivian, you have more important things to do. *We*, Vivian," Chloe said intensely, "we have more important things to do, and death is not one of them."

Gwen asked foolishly, "Who are you?"

"Your sister's dead, Vivian," she said, sharpening the gaze.

"I don't have a sister."

"Her name was Gabby, and she was murdered a few days ago."

Chloe inched even closer.

In return, Gwen took another step away from Chloe.

"If you don't believe me, just look into my eyes," she said as she stepped closer to Gwen. Just feet away now. "Go on," she said. "*Look*."

She focused on that strange light wrapped in Chloe's eyes.

"What is this?" Gwen said, squinting. "What are you doing?"

"Don't fight it," Chloe said.

The light cut through Gwen's eyes.

To Gwen, it felt as if she had a withered door locked inside her mind, and now it was splintering and squeaking as it thrust itself open.

"What are you doing to me?" she said faintly.

"I'm showing you the truth," Chloe said, her eyes widening.

The strange light flooded Gwen's thoughts. They were no longer racing—the thoughts—as they almost always were. They were calm now, focused. The light finally dampened, and a man stepped from a dark corridor. He was a tall man, blonde highlights, handsome. The light broke free in her mind, now filling with manmade structures, a stale room, surgical instruments on a tray, other men and women dressed in white clothes, circling around one person. That person was a woman, a brunette who was seated on a hospital bed, her legs spread open like a door. The woman was screaming and pushing out something. Then, Gwen realized, she was pushing out her and her sister, Gabby.

Two tiny lights, Gwen saw, concealed by a gray shawl. There was another woman in the room as well. She was a nurse, but she wasn't one of the good ones. Something strange about the nurse. Something sinister. . .

Gwen pulled away from Chloe.

"Get out," she said. "Now. . ."

"You're not alone," Chloe said to Gwen. "There's a world beyond those mountains, Vivian. . ."

A grimace rippled through Gwen's face.

"Get the fuck out of my home," she seethed, "or I'm calling the police."

Chloe's shoulder deflated. She looked around the apartment and then shot a glance to the balcony outside.

"If you change your mind, I'm staying in the hotel across the street called the Landmark Inn," Chloe said as she made her way to the door. "Only then will I tell you who I really am."

Chloe left the apartment and then Gwen broke down and cried.

– 1 1 . 1 6 . 2 0 4 8 –

"WHY didn't she go with you?" Mark asked Chloe.

Chloe replied, "Vivian already made up her mind earlier that day. There was no backing out. Death was her only escape."

"Do you think it had anything to do with Gabby's death?"

"I thought about that," Chloe said. "Maybe she knew about Gabby. Maybe a part of Vivian had died. When I gazed her, I never saw that. I saw a woman who was sick and tired of being alone, and there was only one solution to her problem."

"Why didn't you tell the others?"

Chloe replied, "The last thing I wanted to tell them was that their sister didn't want to live anymore. They needed hope even if there was no such thing."

—

CHLOE stepped into the hotel room where Sally was sleeping in the bed, while Juliet was sleeping on the couch.

Juliet, who was still recovering from the gunshot, woke.

"How'd it go?" she asked.

Chloe said bitterly, "I'll try again tomorrow."

—

WHILE Sally and Juliet were sleeping, Chloe kept watch outside on the balcony. She had a clear sight at Gwen's apartment.

The lights were off, and they had been off for the past two hours.

Another hour passed when Chloe saw two flashes of gunfire coming from Gwen's apartment window.

Chloe rose from her seat and peered closer at the window.

There was another flash of gunfire!

Part of the figure was lit up from the gunfire. A man in a dark suit—Chloe saw—had a pistol pointed at another figure whom she assumed was Gwen.

Chloe rushed from the hotel and raced across the street to Gwen's apartment building. . .

There was nobody at the main entrance as there was before—only a few people walking on the sidewalk, but none of them were residents or employees of the apartment.

She found a metal trashcan on the street and flung it through the door. She nicked her hand on the sharp glass as she entered through the broken door, but she ignored the minor injury and kept on going. The security guard had been shot dead, she saw, his body lying to the right of the front counter. Three bullets were used. Two in the chest, and one between the eyes to keep him from retaliating. A classic triple tap. A puddle of blood had already formed around his body, and it was fresh too from the way it funneled through the cracks in the tile.

She took the elevator to Gwen's floor.

When Chloe arrived at her apartment, the door was halfway open.

Chloe cautiously entered.

All six senses were jacked.

Her body felt as if it was vibrating. The gaze was something awful too—powerful enough to pierce through a wall, if the wall had eyes. She listened closely to the darkness, the hum of an air conditioner; and finally, over the hum, she heard the sounds of a woman gagging on her own blood.

She hurried to the bedroom where the sounds were more evident.

Gwen was lying on the floor and gripping the wound on her neck.

"Vivian. . ."

Chloe ran to Gwen and tried to stop the bleeding.

The bullets had missed main organs; however, one bullet had caught an artery. Chloe wondered if it was because of the darkness of the room or if Vivian had gazed one of the shooters and forced the shooter to miss. If that was the case and the shooter *was* somehow gazed, then the shooter must've witnessed the triple tap. Otherwise, he would've never left the victim alive. No chance in hell. The shooter would've watched her take her last breath—if the shooter was the real deal. But why, Chloe wondered as she kneeled down to her sister, why would she want the shooter to miss a kill shot considering she was about to kill herself the other night?

Both of her eyes were still intact too, as far as she could tell. Same with her tongue. It was still there.

She suddenly grabbed Chloe's bloody hand, the one with the gash, and squeezed it tightly.

That was when it happened.

Chloe would later call it a *game changer. . .*

– 1 1 . 1 6 . 2 0 4 8 –

CHLOE didn't quite know if it was because Gwen's blood had gotten into her bloodstream when she grabbed her hand or if it was from the rush of adrenaline after her brush with death. She didn't know what the fuck was inside her, inside Gwen, and she couldn't try to explain it (it was like trying to understand the ins and outs of one's genetic makeup, the certain genetic disorders, the certain mutations, and then use certain methods to prevent one's self from sickness); but what she did know was that these bastards wanted to use her power for other reasons—what reasons exactly, Chloe had no idea. Whatever it was, it couldn't be good. But what other choice did she have? All Chloe knew was what she felt, and Chloe felt it—*still did*—like a current of electricity moving through her veins, the second she touched Gwen's hand. It came and went, this power. She described it as a game changer because it was simply that, a game changer. The Company referenced it as the *gori*, short for upalgorit. The technical term alone was way over her head, even when they tried to explain it to Chloe. In the *Gori for Dummies* version, whoever possessed the gori could access every electronic device connected to the Internet. She just figured it was another ability the gaze had offered her, which it was— and what an ability it was!

"How did it feel to harness this new power for the first time?" Mark asked again.

"Painful," Chloe said, "like no pain I've ever experienced."

She paused for a moment.

(*For a second, she jerked her hand away from Gwen's as if she had gotten shocked. The shock still stayed with her even after she removed her hand—a strange pain moving throughout her entire body. She stared at Gwen with an expression of both pain and pleasure; and that was when Gwen knew, or at least Chloe thought she knew. She couldn't help but ask herself if she had grabbed her hand on purpose or if she just wanted someone or something tangible to hold. Chloe decided it was best not to burden her with the question.*)

Chloe said to Mark, "Eventually, the pain subsided. It felt natural, as if it was there the whole time."

—

SHE ignored the strange sensation, as well as that question, and applied more pressure on the wound.

"Hang in there," she said to Gwen, who was now calm from Chloe's company.

"I saw him, you know," Gwen said, "your father, our father."

"You did?"

Gwen uttered while she coughed up blood, "When I looked into... your eyes.   He was... he was a good man..."

"Why didn't you come with me sooner?"

"Be... cause I saw the world that you spoke of and there was nothing but death in it for me... *for us...*"

"Please..."

"It's better this way, Chloe... this world... it's not meant for us..."

She tightened her grip around Chloe's hand.

Gwen's eyes suddenly bolted open.

"This is the way it's supposed to be..."

"You're wrong."

"We carry death inside us... and you must be the one to destroy them... you're strong..."

"Please, Vivian," Chloe begged.   "Let me get you to a hospital."

Gwen's eyes glazed over.

"My name was Vivian..."

Then, her eyes swam around her head.

She didn't answer Chloe.

"Vivian?"

Chloe checked the pulse on the side of her neck and then her wrist, but she could barely find one on either vein.

She grabbed her face and shook it.

"Stay with me," she said to Gwen.

Her eyes bolted back open.   Then, her eyelids became weak and heavy.

"You have to do it or else... or else I will..."

"Do what?"

"Kill me... it must be *you...*"

Any doubt Chloe had about Gwen *not* wanting to die was put to an end.

In that moment, Chloe gazed Gwen and saw what she really wanted.

But there was something more to it, Chloe saw, *not* just from what Gwen wanted but what the world wanted.

(*Many years from now, this moment would come back to her. Like the other moments Chloe carried inside her, this one right here would be the one to make a difference. . . this was going to be the icebreaker. . .*)

Chloe couldn't help but wonder if there was another side to the gaze, one that she had not yet learned—the ability to see *not* only the thoughts of another person and be able to manipulate certain ones (to project was one ability Chloe had mastered over the past few months, meaning to reanimate her own appearance through another person's thoughts), but also to see into the eyes of the future.

"Do it," Gwen moaned. "You have to. . . "

She had to. She knew. Chloe looked around the dark room and found a shiny object with a sharp point. The object was a clock made of glass. She grabbed the clock from the nightstand. It was sturdy too and she knew it wouldn't break on impact.

Once more, she gazed her and witnessed a desperate woman who would—as soon as she walked away—find that blade resting on the kitchen counter and drive it through her heart. And Gwen would do everything in her power to make sure Chloe *saw* her death, for her to watch her agony fade away, for her to watch the life drain from her eyes. It had to be done.

And Gwen did *not* want to die that way, certainly not by her own hands.

She'd rather put the hardship on this woman, Chloe Dorsey, who was meant to carry the burden with her once more.

Chloe kneeled down over Gwen and straddled her torso and raised the clock above her head.

As the clock towered above Chloe's head, she drove the sharp end through Gwen's face.

One strike.

Two deaths.

— 1 1 . 1 6 . 2 0 4 8 —

"WHY did you really do it?"

Chloe grimaced.

"I did it because I *had* to."

"Why?" Mark asked. "Why, Chloe? You could've stopped the bleeding. You could've saved her from death."

"I know I could, but I didn't," she said. "Vivian's death had a higher meaning."

"And what meaning was that?"

"I don't know yet," Chloe said. "But soon. . . I will."

"How certain are you?"

"More than I've ever been."

—

PEOPLE had started to gather around the front of the apartment building.

Some of them were pointing at Chloe as she prowled her way through the main lobby. Chloe didn't pay any attention to the spectators outside. She was still trying to wrap her head around what had just happened in Gwen's apartment. It wasn't the way Gwen went out. It was what she *saw* before she drove that sharp object through her skull. She tried to make sense of the images, hundreds of them, thousands, all scrambled in her mind—like bad television reception. She only caught bits and pieces of the images, just enough to pique her curiosity.

A clamor of noise pulled Chloe from her racing thoughts.

The noise, Chloe heard, sounded like gibberish; and it was high in pitch and playing rapidly, as if she was pressing a fast forward button.

As she left the building, she focused on the two police officers who tried to apprehend her.

Bad mistake for the officers.

Not Chloe.

After she finished disabling the officers with only a couple of blows, she searched around the crowd and gazed each person as if it was a game of tag. She did this for about two minutes until she finally found the person who witnessed the two people involved in Gwen's shooting. He was local man with a flip phone pressed to his ear. He was frantically pacing outside the crowd. Both of his eyes were moving every which way, but she steadied the gaze, accessed his primary auditory cortex, which dealt with hearing—this, of all skills required in accessing was the trickiest; it was like carefully inserting a piece of thread into the eye of a sewing needle, and she only had one chance at it. If she missed, the man ran a high risk of losing his hearing. He was talking to the police, she heard as she listened to the conversation. That was when she delved *just* a little farther into his mind, now accessing his cerebral cortex. She accessed the visual information: *two men rushing from Gwen's apartment building five minutes ago. They were dressed in black, both of them were carrying guns. They got into a black SUV.* There was another one in the backseat, she saw, but she could not see his face, the local man could not see his face. However, he saw the license plate, and it was there in his brain; however, the number had gotten lost in translation.

But it was there, nonetheless, for her to access: AI 5412.

Chloe erased the past six minutes of the man's memory, from the time the man arrived on Queen's Road Central to the time he nearly got trampled by the two men with guns. The man saw the license plate as the car fled from the scene; but to him, it was just another license plate that didn't have any significance to it.

With the license plate number in mind, Chloe made her way through the crowd and tried to find a car.

She spotted one, a taxi with the engine running.

The driver was on the sidewalk as well, trying to figure out what the commotion was all about.

As Chloe was about to enter the taxi, she was suddenly left at a standstill from a stoplight above. The light flashed red. Nothing unusual about that. Her eyes were drawn to the red light in particular. She squinted at first from the sensitivity. She jarred her body upright! The pain, *Chloe felt*, familiar. The red light spliced with other lights on the street, narrowing like red blades of grass, and then suddenly another jolt of pain. The red lights burgeoned over her entire range of vision until the red light was *inside* her. The light sent a cold and tingly sensation through her veins. Chloe's eyes penetrated the light—going deeper now—beyond its illumination, beyond its source, and into the entire grid of Hong Kong. She saw each stoplight, each road, and each computer. It was like hovering over a sea of lights, millions of them flickering in their own alien way.

And in that sea of light, she found a license plate: AI 5412.

Next, she found a road, Li Yuen Street West.

She honed in on the street, that number, AI 5412. There was a surveillance camera outside a jewelry shop. The black SUV sped across the sight of the camera.

Chloe traced her thoughts back to that one stoplight, the one before her, and like a GPS, a mental marker was placed exactly where the SUV was located.

A loud gasp pulled her from the light, now the red vanishing from her eyes. . .

She took a moment to catch her breath. There was a deadened pain in her eyes as well; and when she rubbed her eyes for a moment, the pain went away. The feeling that she felt was like two fingers pinching one side of her brain.

Eventually, the pinching stopped, and Chloe proceeded after the SUV.

—

THE shooter was stopped at a red stoplight, his eyes occasionally passing the rear view mirror.

At another pass, his eyes caught a taxi speeding directly at them.

And it wasn't stopping!

He suddenly gunned the SUV around the traffic.

Chloe rammed the right side of the bumper, causing part of it to fall off. The SUV spun out of control and then crashed into the window of a Toys N' More. There were a couple of shoppers inside. They immediately scattered and scurried from the store as soon as they heard the booming crash of glass. Some of it rained down on one of the employees of the toy store and left him with minor injuries.

The passenger stumbled out of the SUV and emptied a magazine into the taxi, which had stalled on the sidewalk.

Chloe ducked from the flying bullets and managed to get the engine started again. She put the gear in reverse and floored it. She sped down a sidewalk for another block, knocking over several signs and posts along the way. Chloe finally drove onto the street, zigzagging around cars, parked or idled, and then rammed a couple of them.

The SUV managed to drive from the wreckage and out of the store.

As they chased after Chloe, they ended up running over a couple of pedestrians.

Over a dozen police cars and vans with 警 *Police* 察 written on the side arrived at the scene and joined the pursuit.

———

CHLOE couldn't shake them.

The streets were way too narrow. The traffic was way too congested.

The only option Chloe had was to ditch the taxi.

She drove down an alleyway, which was about as wide as a hallway, until a market prevented her from driving any farther.

The SUV was forced to park outside the alleyway, but Chloe still gained enough distance from them to give herself a chance.

Now, on foot, Chloe moved the chase through the late night markets, as well as the never-ending street crowds.

The vibrant colors from street level to the garish signs, billboards, and marquees suspended above and the plethora of smells and the ambience of sounds were intoxicating, and at the same time, disorientating. There were traders everywhere she turned; and they had everything from black market goods to every type of ware stolen from big name retailers (it was as if a spam bomb exploded all on this one street). There were many fortune-tellers as well—one dressed in a loud pink and white garment, yelling something in what Chloe thought was in tongues. She cut into another alley and then another. One wrong turn forced Chloe down darker alleyways, which were packed with darker goods, cheaper ware, prostitutes, drug dealers, hovels, a narrow strip of squalid restaurants which bled into congested streets—the steam rising from corroded barbeques was making it hard to breath. Food—eat at one's own risk—was the last thing on her mind, even though the smell was everywhere she turned. She even came across a trader who was selling every flavor of pornography, which was illegal in most countries. Chloe passed a waste bin of old DVD's repackaged and sealed in loose plastic. What Chloe saw inside one of them made her queasy to the stomach; snuff films, she saw, torture porn, the kind of shit that would make any person queasy to the stomach. But that—surprisingly enough—wasn't what made her queasy. One of them, Chloe saw, was a softcore porno with the actress, Kaia Ganguly. Chloe knew the name from her father's CD, studied the name, *recited* the name. The name of the movie was *Hunt Her Down*. Chloe took a double take of the movie, and realized the actress was *not* Kaia, only a look-alike pretending to be Kaia.

She made it to another street where there was another market, this one a little more appropriate. There was no escaping the sounds of police sirens, now blaring all around her.

The two shooters were closing in on her as well.

She decided to lure them into a quieter place, which was hard to find around here—since every little thing had a pulse. She took cover behind a trader's stand (he was selling necklaces, but nobody was buying them) and waited for the two to make their way around the corner.

As soon as one of them did (the second one lagging behind), Chloe gazed him. He had two weapons, a knife in his left hand, a gun in the other. She never turned his body to stone, at least not the part a normal person could see on the outside. His head started to become heavy. He clutched a post with one hand and grabbed the side of his head with the other.

Then, it suddenly happened, the impossible. . . Each orifice of the man's face oozed with strings of blood. His head flopped to the ground, taking his body with him. His entire brain—once made of soft nervous tissue—now as hard as stone.

The man died instantly.

But there were still two left, including the mystery man.

One, she remembered, perhaps the man in charge, waiting in the SUV.

Trying to catch her breath from the recent gaze, she kept her eyes open for the next one.

As soon as she turned her shoulder, she found him rounding a corner. The man made eye contact with Chloe, and she made eye contact with him. She had depleted most of her energy by gazing the other one, which was the longest distance Chloe had ever gazed another person before.

The man aimed the gun at Chloe when suddenly a police officer yelled out from across an alleyway, "*Dòngjié* (Freeze)!"

A gunshot suddenly rang out; however, it didn't come from the man who had a gun pointed at Chloe.

Chloe quickly ducked back into a crowd of people before the other officers arrived on the scene.

While the police officers moved the spectators away from the deceased body, Chloe made it back to the street without getting spotted.

As she rounded another corner, she saw that same SUV driving by.

It didn't stop, though.

Yet, it kept driving along at the legal speed limit.

The man behind the steering wheel shot a glance at Chloe as he drove by.

In that moment, Chloe saw her father, not behind the steering wheel of the SUV, but in the man's eye.

Chloe was no longer standing on the sidewalk, no longer in Hong Kong for that matter.

Instead, she was cowered under a desk in an office. A wall of fire was growing all around her. She realized it was *not* her who was cowered under the desk. It was him, but it wasn't him. He was a young boy at the time. The man in the SUV had carried these thoughts with him as long as he could remember.

As brief as the moment was in the passing of their eyes, she went deeper into his thoughts.

(*A tall man was strutting through the towering flames. The boy's father was telling his son to keep quiet, using a finger held in front of his mouth to indicate the severity of the situation, and, that no matter what happened or what he heard, to stay under the desk. There were other children there as well. Each one of them was hiding from her father, Freeze.*

Chloe saw him, *her father*, and then she heard the screaming.

She pulled herself from the driver and caught her breath.

– 1 1 . 1 6 . 2 0 4 8 –

"PLEASE clarify, Chloe," Mark said. "Why didn't Vivian leave Hong Kong after you came to see her?"

"The same reason why I stayed at USR for so damn long."

"And why was that?"

Mark placed the tablet aside.

"Because she was trapped," Chloe said. "That's why."

Mark replied, "Eventually, you quit your job at USR. If you hadn't, you would've never known what you know now."

"The first time I gazed Vivian," Chloe said over a sigh, "I saw what I would've looked like in four years, better job, yes, more friends, perhaps, but there was this void deep inside her, and it had gotten so big and so dark and so empty that there was no possible way it could've been filled with anything meaningful."

"You mean love?"

"Yes," she said. "Even love. Vivian was lost in a world that she created for herself. And whenever she felt the least amount of anything for someone or something, she'd find that darkness before it found her."

"With that said, how did it feel to harness this new power for the first time?"

—

CHLOE made it back to Landmark Inn.

Both Juliet and Sally were sound asleep, despite all of the commotion outside the hotel.

Chloe rushed into Sally's room.

"Get up," Chloe shook Sally on the shoulder, "we have to go. . ."

Juliet slowly woke from Chloe's voice.

"What's wrong?" she said from the doorway.

Chloe didn't respond to Juliet's remark.

Frantically, she gathered all of Sally's things and stuffed them in a duffel bag.

"Chloe!" Juliet said, louder. "Answer me!"

"I don't have time to explain," she said, paying little attention to Juliet. "Get your things! We have to leave!"

Juliet saw the blood on Chloe's hands, as well as her shirt.

"You're bleeding," she said. "Are you hurt?"

Chloe didn't even notice the blood, not until Juliet had said something about it. She stopped what she was doing and looked down at her hands and saw Vivian's blood on them. There was a cut too from where her hand nicked sharp glass. Chloe needed stitches—maybe—but it was nothing that superglue couldn't fix.

"Chloe. . . what happened. . ."

She continued to pack Sally's things, a shirt and then a dolly draped over the pillow.

"Chloe!" Juliet cried out.

In return, Chloe shouted out, "I said 'Get your things!'"

The two remained quiet, Sally on the verge of tears.

Chloe finally stopped.

She placed the duffel bag aside and sauntered to the window.

"Vivian's dead," she said softly as she glanced outside the hotel.

The police were gathering around the front of the apartment building.

"What?" Juliet said from behind. "How?"

"It's doesn't matter now," she said and faced the other two. "Do you trust me?"

Juliet didn't answer.

Chloe moved her eyes toward Sally.

"Sally?"

"I trust you, Chloe," she said.

Next, she looked at Juliet.

"Yes," she said. "Of course."

Chloe said, "Then, let's get out of here."

— 1 1 . 1 6 . 2 0 4 8 —

"HAVE you seen any of her films?"

"A couple," Chloe said. "I saw them on the Internet."

"Any good?" Mark asked.

"Yeah," she said with a shrug. "Not bad."

CAPE TOWN, SOUTH AFRICA
JUNE 23, 2015

THE Majora Theatre at the Orange Point Film Festival was the one place where actors, critics, and film aficionados could all come together under the same roof.

Kaia Ganguly was one of those people. . .

In the film, *the handsome renegade, Antigo, was trying to justify his brother Omar's recent imprisonment and at the same time, trying to nurture the wounded starlet who was Madi, Omar's former lover.*

The sound of the oceans waves crashing against the shore caused the tears to run from her eyes.

"We are all like chickens in a coop," Antigo told Madi, "waiting to die. The question, Madi: 'When will our own Bill rise to the occasion and test our fate?' When, or if that time comes, will we fight like Omar did or will we die?"

The screen faded to black.

A soft composition played over the blackness, which sounded something similar to Mozart's "Requiem in D Minor."

Next, the credits rolled over the blackness.

A thunderous uproar filled the entire audience, a combination of clapping and whistling. Kaia's date for the screening, as well as her longtime friend, Fin Normandy, a producer whom she met on the set of an indie film shot in upstate New York, reached over and kissed Kaia on the cheek.

"Beautiful," he whispered in her ear.

"Thank you, Fin," Kaia said, her face slack and tired but held nicely together with a layer of makeup.

—

THINGS were going well on the night of June 23rd until Chloe decided to crash the party.

Kaia went to excuse herself to the ladies restroom when suddenly a door closed behind her.

The restroom was rather dark, but it was clean and made presentable for the guests.

It wasn't the closing of the door that bothered Kaia. It was the fact that the person who followed her into the ladies' room locked the door after it was closed.

Kaia saw a younger woman standing behind her in the reflection of the mirror.

A dim fluorescent light above was flickering—as if either the electrician didn't install the bulb correctly or it was running off its last surge of electricity.

"May I help you?" Kaia asked, gripping her purse.

She could hardly make out the stranger who was standing behind her.

That stranger was none other than Chloe, and she didn't say a word to Kaia. Not at first.

Didn't have to.

Kaia rotated around.

They both shared a long stare. A gaze.

Kaia said suddenly, "How did you find me?"

"Your agent."

"Where are the others?"

"They're in a secure location not far from here, but you already know that."

— 1 1 . 1 6 . 2 0 4 8 —

MARK asked Chloe, "How did Ms. Ganguly recognize you?"

She answered, "Kaia had the gaze too. Didn't even know she had it, but she did." She paused for a moment and cleared her throat. "When we first met in Cape Town, it was like I didn't have to explain who I was or why I was there to her. She already knew. Everything. It was like. . ." Chloe paused, ". . . like she had a locked door inside her mind, and it was guarded by these," she searched for the right word until it came to her, "*characters*," she said, "characters she created throughout her acting career."

(Standing in the ladies' room, her eyes aimed at Kaia's, Chloe saw them behind Kaia's eyes. There were so many faces, so many lies. She went deeper and saw one woman in particular. Her face was heavily scarred; her skin was smooth and thin and waxy and pink. That woman was named Sashay, and she was not real. She was a character created by a screenwriter named Whitney Tucker, a member of the Guild. But to Kaia, she was real. Her husband had burned her face with acid after she disobeyed his commands. The film was called Scarred, and it had won a couple of independent awards.)

"When I gazed Kaia," Chloe said, "she didn't even know that she was gazing me. I pushed aside all of these characters, these faces that she carried inside her, and I opened that door and that was when I saw it. . . "

"What did you see?" Mark asked.

"Horror," she said, "so much horror, and it was shaped like a spool of yarn. It was alive like an organism. For all these years, she had been carrying around this. . . this one organ. It was self-created. Yet, she couldn't tell the difference from what was real and what was not. The only thing that was real was the person standing in front of her. I. . . I was real."

SANTA ANA, EL SALVADOR
AUGUST 20, 2015

THERE were still a few hours of daylight outside.

They happened to be passing through the second largest city of El Salvador when a team of agents came barging into the safe house.

Their faces had been plastered across the entire continent of South America and all of its countries, as well as Central America.

"*¡Ya están aquí* (They're here!)*!*" shouted Diego as he scurried away from the window.

Three armored SUVs—black with tinted windows—were parked outside.

Both Sophia and Emilio scrambled into the kitchen and then grabbed the weapons from the table.

Agents rushed from the vehicles. Diego caught a glimpse of them. They were dressed like the SUVs, in black: black masks with tinted visors, nothing written on their backs.

No FBI.

No POLICÍA.

Just black.

One agent in particular stood out the most. He was sporting a black suit without armor, at least none that could be seen on the outside. He was bald as well, not bald because he had lost all of his hair, but bald because he chose to be bald. He had a stony face, bold skeletal structure, with a finely trimmed beard, which was full and shaved to a half-inch every other day.

His name was Agent Noble; and for some reason, Diego knew he was important.

However, Diego didn't plan on going out that quietly.

—

THEY didn't stand a chance.

They were outnumbered from the very start.

All three of them.

Even with what Diego possessed, there were way too many of them.

The agents killed Emilio first and then Sophia, who went out in a blaze of gunfire.

They had Diego cornered in a hallway, but he reminded himself that he wasn't going out that quietly.

He took out a couple of agents with a shotgun, but they kept coming. He threw down the empty shotgun, grabbed the head of Agatha, and inserted a live grenade inside her mouth.

"You want it," Diego said, as Agent Noble shouldered his way through a team of agents and approached Diego. "Come and get it."

"Put down the head, Mr. Tovar," Agent Noble said as he ordered the agents to lower their M4A1s.

They did as commanded and lowered the assault rifles.

Agent Noble holstered the pistol and said calmly to Diego, "It's over, *hombre*. . ."

—

WITH his eyes wide and crazy, Diego seethed, "*Vete a la chingada* (Go fuck yourself). . ."

Diego pulled the pin.

A couple of other agents rushed toward Diego and tried to remove the grenade from Agatha's gaping mouth, but it was too far crammed inside.

The grenade went off, instantly killing Diego, as well as *most* of the agents who tried to pry it from the mouth.

Agent Noble happened to be one of those agents.

PART TWO

A WEEK WITH DEATH

THEY decided to take a break after the first day of cataloging and start back early the next morning after Chloe received her eight hours of sleep.

No more.

No less.

Three lanky guards dressed in protective gear entered what was known as the "white room," a designated room where the cataloging was being conducted. One guard was holding a cup of coffee in a silver mug without a handle. The others were carrying wands, charged and ready to be put to use if she got out of line. Chloe called them zappers, and they hurt like hell. She had been on the wrong end of one a few times, mainly the first days spent in Death Valley, and that—for damn sure—was one pain she'd never forget.

They brought her coffee at the same time they did yesterday and placed it in front of her.

Clockwork.

The guard removed the electronic shackles from both of her wrists with a sensor and exited the white room.

The other two guards exited as well.

Now, Chloe was alone.

The room was silent, except for a soft hum coming from the bright white walls as if the walls thrummed with strange energy.

Chloe picked up the cup of coffee, raised it to her nose, and breathed in the steam. She lowered her head and took a sip, cautiously at first, to test out the heat. It was the same temperature as it was yesterday.

Perfect.

She took another sip, larger this time, and held the coffee in her mouth and savored each note and spice.

The beans, as she was told, had come from somewhere in Indonesia, and were like no beans Chloe had ever tasted.

She slowly removed her sharp eyes from the steam and moved them upward, only to witness Mark seated in front of her.

The first question: "How is it?"

Startled from Mark's presence, Chloe swallowed the sip and said modestly, "It's okay."

"Just okay," Mark replied vacantly.

"Yeah." Chloe shrugged. "It's the only thing I look forward to in this hamster cage."

"Shall we begin?"

She took another sip of coffee.

There was an aftertaste, she noticed as she removed the mug from her face. It was so faint, and yet her sense of taste was unlike that of any normal person. Chloe couldn't put a name on it, on the aftertaste, even though it tasted almost. . . synthetic.

"I take that as a yes."

After she took yet another sip, she shot a glance at the large mirror beside her. She didn't think she showed it to them, but she did. To the naked eye, the gesture could've easily gone unnoticed. They could detect these kinds of things, even if it was as discrete or mundane as a slight twitch on the lower left corner of her mouth.

Behind the mirror: *Let's wipe that smirk off her face.*

Mark acknowledged the whispery voice in his ear with two blinks of his eyelids.

Mark said to Chloe, "You found Ms. Ganguly, the old-est, in Cape Town. Is that correct?"

"Yeah," she said flatly, more interested in the coffee.

"How long did you stay in Cape Town?"

"Not long," she answered. "Only a day before they found us. And there were more of them too, twice as many as there were in Hong Kong."

"How many?"

"Six, I believe, including Rake."

Chloe sipped from the coffee.

"They forced us south," she said. "We managed to hop on a cargo vessel. We didn't have a clue where it was go-ing. We were left with no other choice than to wait it out until the ship reached its destination. It gave us time to recover as well. The girls were exhausted, especially with all the running around we were doing. Kaia took it the hardest."

"Why?" Mark asked.

"It's not everyday that you get to dodge bullets for a liv-ing," she said. "Real bullets. Not squibs, as she called them. Think she was still waiting for the director to pop out somewhere and yell, 'Cut.' We stopped at an island, the Falkland Islands, just south of Argentina. We knew we had to find a way off the island because we didn't stand a chance here—knowing they were right on our tails. We had to get inland. South America was where we needed to be. We figured if we made it to South America, then—if we kept our heads down for a little while—maybe there was still a chance for us."

"Do you blame yourself for their deaths?"

Chloe didn't answer.

Mark blinked twice.

"Do you blame yourself for their deaths, Chloe?"

"Yes."

"Why?"

Chloe said abruptly, "I was supposed to protect them. They looked up to me. And I let them down."

"Where were you when Sally was murdered?"

"We made it inland." Chloe sighed. "We stopped in Trelew to rest for a couple of days."

"Did you have any particular destination once you reached Argentina?"

"No." She sipped from the coffee. "At that point, we had to keep going north. *Moving was living.* They didn't find us until we arrived in Buenos Aires."

"How did it happen?"

Chloe said, "I went out to grab some food. I was gone for ten minutes, not even that long. When I got back, Sally was gone. Both Kaia and Juliet were unconscious."

"Why didn't they kill them?"

"Instead of them trying to take us out at the same time, they got smarter and picked us off one at a time." Chloe shook her head in disgust. "Sally was first."

"Was it because she was the youngest?"

"Maybe," she said. "I don't know."

"What happened next?"

(*Chloe charged from the hostel while Juliet and Kaia stayed behind with the doors locked. They were still re-covering from the sudden blows to their heads. They never killed them, though, as Chloe would later explain to Mark.*

She surveyed the grungy street teeming with late night partygoers, but Sally was nowhere to be found.

From a distance, Chloe heard the screech of tires.

Next, a car skidding onto a side road. . .)

"I chased after them. . ." Chloe said.

(*The last she saw of the car, after the chase throughout a compact district where the roads were as tight as an al-ley, was two red brake lights and then the car speeding away from a landfill.*)

". . . When I found Sally, I knew it was the same people who killed Gabby."

(*Chloe rushed from the car and down a hill covered in garbage and debris. Somewhere amidst the trash was a dead body, recently killed. Nobody would ever find it too, her body, if Chloe hadn't found it—the smell was beyond grotesque, but nobody would find her. But Chloe did. She stumbled down the hill and finally made it to the body. She realized it was Sally the moment she turned over the body and saw her little face. Both of her eyes had been gouged out. Her throat. . . slit.*

Chloe held Sally's body close to hers and never wanted to let go, ever.)

Her eyes watered from the thought of young Sally and what these monsters had done to her.

"She was just a little girl, and she was tossed away like a piece of garbage."

"How did it make you feel?"

"How do you think it made me feel?"

"Upset?"

"Upset?" Chloe said angrily. "I think *upset* is an understatement."

"What did you do with the body?"

"I burned it," she said. "Kept a handful of ashes."

"Why?"

"To *remind* me what I was up against."

"How did the others take it?"

"Juliet," Chloe said, "Juliet took it the hardest. She and Sally had become close during our time together."

"How did you take it, Chloe?"

She thought about Mark's question, but not for too long.

She said, "I couldn't let them see me like that. I had to stay strong."

———

"WHAT are you feeling right now?"

"Weak," Chloe said. "I feel weak."

"Do you ever believe that things happen for a reason?"

"What exactly is that supposed to mean?" Chloe said defensively. "Are you saying I was supposed to be locked up in this hellhole, that *this*, this was my destiny?"

Mark didn't answer.

"Is that what you're saying?"

"Why did you take Juliet's death the hardest?"

(They were closing in on the last SUV; though, she never got used to driving on these roads. They were driving on a narrow street in a small town in Colombia.

"I see her," Kaia cried out as Chloe tried to dodge each pedestrian on the side of the street.

One of the kidnappers was doing something to her, Kaia noticed. Juliet, however, was putting up a fight.

One of the passenger windows was suddenly kicked out.

"She's struggling, Chloe," Kaia said urgently to Chloe.

"I'm driving as fast as I can!" Chloe shouted back.

"Hurry!"

Chloe followed, "I am!"

Then, they watched it happen. . .)

"I was caught off guard. . ."

(The back door of the SUV opened as Chloe and Kaia closed in. They got right on the bumper, just feet away from touching it.

One of these "supposed" agents dragged Juliet's slack body from the backseat and tossed her body at the Jeep behind them.

Chloe saw every frame, as if Juliet was flying in slow motion. Her lifeless body went directly through the Jeep's windshield—head first—causing Chloe to swerve off the street.)

"Caught off guard?" Mark said. "Was it because they did the same thing they did to Sally and Gabby?"

"No."

(Chloe slammed on the brakes, got out of the car, and pulled the body from the windshield.

As with Sally, Juliet was missing both of her eyes. Her throat was slit too, but she was still clinging onto her last breath. She went into shock from the loss of blood. Chloe tried to resuscitate Juliet, but she had already lost too much blood.)

"Then why, Chloe?"

(Kaia yelling from the Jeep: "Come on! She's dead, Chloe! We have to go!")

"Somehow," she said and sniffled the loose phlegm from her nose, "before they removed her eyes, I managed to gaze Juliet. Just a glimpse. That's all I needed."

"And what did you see?"

"I saw..." Chloe struggled to speak the words, "...I saw a woman who *wanted* to live. She didn't want to die. I saw... I saw that she... she wanted me to save her. Juliet didn't want to die. For months, trapped in that hospital, she wanted to kill herself. She spent all day thinking of ways to do it. Then, after I found her, all those thoughts they..."

"They what?"

"They no longer existed."

Chloe lowered her head and sobbed into her hands.

"She was counting on me, and I failed her."

"Tell me what happened to Kaia?"

Chloe wiped the tears from her eyes.

"Two days later," Chloe said as she caught her breath, "they found Kaia and me just outside Cali. It's like they were watching us the entire time. It was quick, though. Kaia, she wasn't much of a fighter, not like Juliet. They knew that. Her power rested behind her eyes. They knew."

Mark asked, "How did it happen?"

(*Chloe pulled back the curtain and stepped from the shower and suddenly heard a soft thud coming from the bedroom. She grabbed the towel from the hanger and didn't bother drying off. She grabbed her underwear next. She slipped into them, one leg at a time.*

"Kaia," Chloe said as she crept into the bedroom.

She found Kaia sitting in a chair in the middle of the room. Her head was flopped over the headrest. She had a bullet hole in the center of her forehead; and like the others, her eyes had been removed.)

Chloe grimaced.

She asked Mark, "Do we have to do this?"

"Yes." Mark intertwined his fingers. "Continue."

"After they got Kaia," she finally said, "somehow I knew that whoever these people were, they were saving me for last."

"Why did you think that?"

"I didn't know why," she said. "I just knew."

"Because of Mr. Rake?"

"Yeah."

Chloe hung her head.

———

CHLOE sat in her cell.

It was like any other cell. It had a bed. It had a sink. It had a toilet. It had a window too, which was as small as a basement window. Nonetheless, it was a window, and everyday at noon a strange light shone through it and cast a sword-like ray on the plain white wall, which also acted like a projection screen whenever they played a movie for Chloe. They were always oldies— mostly black and whites. Chloe never got to pick. Didn't care. The movies usually put her to sleep.

Maybe that was the whole point. . .

She didn't touch the feed on the plate.

Didn't read the book either. This time it was *Where The Red Fern Grows* by Wilson Rawls.

———

"YOU know, *Mark*," she said, emphasizing the name Mark with what sounded almost like mockery as she peeled a hangnail from the side of her thumb, "I think we should talk more about the book selection."

Mark eyed Chloe's busy fingers, both the thumbs and the index finger, and said strangely, "Not a fan?"

"They're a little too juvenile for my taste."

She stopped picking at the hangnail.

"I don't pick out the books."

Chloe asked, "Then, who does?"

"Shall we begin?"

She said mildly, "Whatever."

Mark placed the tablet on the table.

"I'm surprised you haven't asked me about him."

"About who?"

"You know. . . Diego. . . "

"Are you referring to Diego Tovar?"

"What other Diego would I be talking about?"

"Mr. Tovar is no longer an interest to JeneCorp."

"But you do know what happened to him. Right?"

"Yes," she said. "I heard. I hear everything. Remember?"

Mark pressed the tablet's touch screen and pulled up the last conversation he and Chloe had, about Kaia's death.

Chloe asked, "What did you people do with Diego?"

"That's not how the cataloging works," Mark said. "I ask the questions. You answer them."

"Did you really kill him?"

"I am not authorized to answer that question."

Chloe waited for a legit answer.

"Shall we begin?"

Mark blinked twice, then finally asked Chloe, "Did you ever think about Diego Tovar during your travels throughout South America?"

"I did."

"And?"

"And. . . I never found him," Chloe said. "I just assumed he was already dead."

"Then, why did you promise Mr. Merrotti that you would find him?"

"Next question."

"Very well."

Mark scrolled through the tablet.

"Were you still upset with what Diego had done to your father?"

"Of course," Chloe said, "but after what happened with the others, what he did seemed like a slap on the wrist. I know he never wanted to hurt my father."

"How so?"

Chloe answered bluntly, "I saw the guilt in his eyes after he threw my father to the floor. It was an accident. Plain and simple."

"How about Mr. Jacobson?" Mark asked. "Was that an accident as well?"

"Renny brought that upon himself. Not Diego."

"So, you defend Mr. Tovar's actions."

"I don't defend Diego," Chloe said. "I never will. There was still a part of me that wanted Diego to ask forgiveness for what he did."

"After all you learned about Mr. Tovar, what he had done to your foster parents, the assassination of President Robert Shaw, you would be willing to forgive a person like that?"

She thought, then answered, "Of all the people out there, he was the only one who opened my eyes. Despite what he did, if it wasn't for Diego, then I would've still been that pathetic woman stuck at that shitty job." She turned the tables and asked Mark, "What kind of fucking life is that?"

Of course, Mark didn't answer.

—

MARK didn't get a response at first.

Mark blinked twice—as he was known to do—and asked the question again, but didn't get anything from Chloe, only a blank stare.

(*Chloe wiped the tears from her eyes and tied a weight around her ankle and jumped off the cliff. The weight helped carry her farther below where the light was no more. Even the water was colder down here, but life, she witnessed, was as brilliant as a rainbow. There was marine life swimming all around her, creatures she had never seen before. They appeared like tiny aliens. She suddenly gazed each life form. The different fish hardened in their swim and slowly sank to the bottom of the ocean floor.*

Jellyfish.

They turned to stone too.
One jellyfish remained.)

"Why that one in particular?" Mark asked.

"I don't know," Chloe answered. "I think it was trying to tell me something."

"Tell you what?"

"It finally came to me, and I realized that this wasn't the way I was supposed to die." She thought about dying a lot. There were many times when she could've ended it. There were many times when she could've just let go, but something strange was holding her back. A force. "I wasn't supposed to die like this," she said to Mark. "I realized that. . . there was another way."

— 1 1 . 1 8 . 2 0 4 8 —

CHLOE told Mark, "They must've lost my trail after I crossed the border of Nicaragua. After I left León— Nicaragua, not Mexico—I spent a couple of months in Guatemala. I made a couple of amigos along the way. Good people. *Great* people. They had a nice place not far from Lake Atitlán. Never have I seen something so majestic. After everything that had happened, I questioned a lot of things. I questioned my existence. Most importantly, I questioned my faith. If there was ah. . . a god out there, a creator who created all of this, why would He do this to me? Why? Why would He make me watch the people I love die all around me? Why. . . why would He put me through so much pain? What was the purpose? For so long. . . I hated Him!"

(Chloe stood in front of a mirror and punched it, causing a spiderweb crack to form over the glass.

She looked down at her hand, all bloody.)

"I wanted to take that jagged piece of glass and stab Him directly in the heart! That is if He even had one! I wanted Him to feel my wrath! Then," she calmed a little, shook the thought from her head, "then. . . He spoke to me. Whatever it was—whoever it was—I heard it, the force. I could feel the breath of this strange force pressed against me and for once in my life, I let the breath inside. I let this. . . cold and yet warm sensation run through my veins, my body. That was when I knew. . . I knew it was all a test. . ."

(*Chloe walked along a winding dirt path, her hand brushing against all the vegetation next to her. She had never seen so many plants, and they were as tall as trees. Leaves as round as her head. She kneeled down along the manmade path, which was a popular biking trail, and fingered a ladybug on the leaf.*)

". . . Every single life form had meaning, purpose. . ."

(*She suddenly flinched from the piercing growl of a black jaguar roaming through the jungle. Her eyes crossed the deadly creature's yellow eyes, the black blades swelling inside them, and then it kept roaming through the jungle.*

And so did Chloe, this time with purpose.)

". . . I had purpose."

(*She sat on the edge of a cliff and peered at the lake, the horizon scribbled with volcanoes. Never had she ever seen a sight so gorgeous.*

A wave of calmness washed over her body, her face.)

"And what was your purpose, Chloe?"

Chloe's eyes sharpened.

"To be sitting here with you. . ."

For a second, silence filled the room.

The only noise came from that steady hum.

Then, Mark said vacantly, "Very good, Chloe." Somewhere beneath that vacant stare, a smile was forming. Chloe couldn't see it, but she could *sense* it.

Once more, Mark said, "Very good."

———

CHLOE sipped from the rest of the coffee.

"When I was on the road," Chloe said to Mark, "there were times when I thought about my father. I thought about Sally, Juliet as well, Vivian, Gabby, *Kaia*." For a second, *just* a second, a smile pulled across her face when she mentioned Kaia's name. "For some reason, I could still feel them inside me."

(*Chloe jumped into a giant sinkhole in the earth. She paddled through the murky water—with the other crea-tures.*)

Mark asked, "How did they make you feel?"

(*She flung back her wet hair, did one quick stroke over the top of her scalp with one hand, and peered at the glassy sky above.*

A sharp beam of sunlight cut through the gaps in the branches.

The light stretched out like an arm, then a hand, then fingers.

Chloe carefully removed her hand from the water and touched the light.)

"Good," Chloe said. "They made me feel good about my-self. They gave me strength."

Her face slackened, eyes too.

(*Her hand lifted over Sally's—her hand so tiny against Chloe's palm.*

They both smiled and laughed.

She removed her hand from Sally's and pointed at the blank spot on her chest.

Sally fell for the trick and drew her eyes to the "spot."

Next, Chloe flipped Sally's chin, causing her to giggle.

Chloe laughed too.

Hadn't laughed so hard in years.)

There was a laugh building somewhere behind her steely face, but it never gathered enough vim or vigor to be released in front of Mark—at least not in its entirety. Only a trace of it mistakenly slipped from the crack of her lip, and it sounded like a muffled snort.

Before the laugh built anymore, it receded back into the hollowness from where it dwelled.

Chloe said, "Sally gave me innocence, only if it was for a moment. Juliet, she showed me what it was like to be strong. And Kaia taught me to see the beauty in things, even if they came in the tiniest forms."

(*Kaia cradled a centipede in both of her hands and then let it crawl its way onto Chloe's hand.*)

"And I thought about Diego," she said. "I thought maybe I would bump into him."

"So, did you ever feel threatened by the idea of bumping into Mr. Tovar?"

"Diego wasn't a threat."

"Go on."

"I stopped at the temple, Tikal. It was much smaller in person. Eventually, I left Guatemala. I had to keep moving. *Moving was living.*"

"Were you ready to come back to the States?"

"I didn't miss it one bit," Chloe admitted, "in fact, I totally forgot what it was like to live in America. I spent about year in Mexico. Moving from one city to another. I was now ready to come back home."

"Do you consider America your home?"

Chloe didn't answer.

Mark asked one more time.

"Yes," she said. "It'll always be home. *Always.*"

—

MARK asked her if she ran into any trouble crossing the US border.

(*She found a group—and little did they know, they were traveling with one of the "Most Wanted" persons in the world. Most of them were younger, teenagers. The elders stayed behind, they told Chloe, because they couldn't make the arduous trip. The conditions were too hard on the body. One of them was just a kid, only twelve years old. At the end of the night and just on the cusp of dawn, they managed to escape a rancher who had shot at them on the Texas border. She never gazed the rancher. Could've. Chloe didn't want to draw any suspicion to herself, so she didn't use the gaze. These guys were good, though. Three of them had tried two times before, got caught, and then got deported back to Mexico. But that never stopped them from trying again. To them, America*) *was an opportunity and a means to support the familia. And that was all these people who traveled with Chloe wanted, an opportunity. That was all. They couldn't find it in Mexico, so they tried elsewhere. They found a hole in the fence and they made it through, except for one, a fifteen-year-old who got shot during the escape.)*

"Not really," she said.

(Seeing the relief on their faces, if only for a short while, was enough to set her mind at ease, just enough to give her—dare she say—a sense of. . . bliss; and yet, she knew that sense of uncertainty would always linger in the back of their minds and that there would once come a day when their asses would be deported back to Mexico, or in her case, to jail. What does a man have to do in order to earn his keep? How far does man have to travel until he is no longer curtailed by the laws set forth by relics? Will we welcome man with open arms or will we shun him from society?)

"The way I looked at it, I was no different than them."

"How so?" Mark asked.

Chloe answered, "They wanted to contribute to society and make a life for themselves."

"Tell me, Chloe," Mark said. "Since you were wanted by the authorities, what exactly did you think you could do to contribute to society? Did you actually think changing your appearance or name would make any difference? Soon, they would find you and when they did, you would go straight to prison."

"Yeah," Chloe said. "I know. I guess there was a part of me that kept telling myself that one day they would stop looking for me, that things would go back to normal. I. . . I was only kidding myself."

"What would you do?" Mark asked. "How would you contribute?"

"I thought I could maybe work as a waitress again or something low key like that," she said. "I didn't mind working as a waitress in Anodes."

"And how did you feel when you came back to America?"

"Apprehensive," she said. "I felt extremely apprehensive."

"Where did you go after you crossed the border?"

She played with her fingers for a minute or so, mostly picking at another hangnail on her thumb.

"Chloe?"

"I followed the eastern edge of the Rocky Mountains until I reached a city called Helena, Montana," she finally answered as she placed her hands aside.

"Did you like Helena?"

"Yes," she said quietly. "I did. It was home."

"What did you like the most about Helena?"

"There was something about it that caught my eye. It was hard to explain. I felt. . . protected. . . "

(*"This is it," she said to the driver as she took a second to absorb the scenery around her.*

She stepped from the truck and grabbed her things from the bed and gazed the Good Samaritan who had given her a lift from Colorado Springs to Helena. And abracadabra! Chloe erased all memory he had of her. As far as the fellow knew, he had decided to get away from the misses and travel to Helena for the weekend

Why Helena?

Well, why not. . .)

"There was a ranch outside Helena," she said. "Mountains all around. Miles and miles of untouched land."

(*She found a rancher, an older man named James Mann. When she gazed James, she saw that he had no children, which was perfect. He once had a partner named Gloria, but Gloria had passed four years ago, which, sad for James, was also perfect. They tried to have children of their own, but Gloria was barren. He had an older sister too. Her name was Bridget, but he hadn't talked to her in years. In fact, they didn't have much of a relationship at all. Bridget lived in Charlotte, North Carolina. She had a family of her own, and ever since James had moved to Montana, he was no longer a part of that family, which was—that's right—perfect; in fact, it was more than perfect. It was the luck of the draw.*

So what did Chloe do?

She gazed James, and now, with a touch of magic, James now had a daughter named Patti Smith. Tina Smith, James's partner before he met Gloria, had given birth to Patti just six months after James left his job and took off to Helena. After Tina passed last year from breast cancer, Patti made it her mission to track down her birth father, James.)

Chloe said, "I changed my name to Patti Smith. There was a house behind the main house. It was the great disguise. *Perfect.* I worked as a waitress at a diner a couple of miles in town. It was exactly what I needed at that stage of my life."

"Were you happy?"

"No," she said. "I wasn't happy. I didn't want to be happy."

"Then what did you want?"

"I didn't want anything."

"Did you ever miss it, living on the run?"

"There were times I missed the thrill of the chase," she said, not missing a beat, "but I was getting older. My body was getting older. I couldn't be that woman. Not anymore. I needed a change."

"How long did you stay in Helena?"

"I lived there for about a year until change found me, *purpose.*"

"Devon Merrotti. Correct?"

It took her a couple of seconds to finally respond.

"That's right."

"How did it feel when you saw Mr. Merrotti?"

"Surprised, for one," she said. "Secondly, I was afraid."

"Why were you afraid of Mr. Merrotti?"

"Because, somehow, in the very back of my mind, I knew that he was going to ask me to do something I didn't want to do."

"How did Mr. Merrotti find you?"

"'The old-fashioned way,' he told me. After he left Jester, Devon said he spent the past two years of his life tracking me down. Spent all this time looking for me when he could've been going after the man who tried to kill him."

(*She came home after a long day of work. A customer spilled a glass of lemonade on her apron, but most of it went down in the hard-to-reach areas on her body and stayed there throughout the entire day, making things a little stickier. James was already in bed, as usual. He crashed around nine after his nightly bowl of corn flakes. He didn't bother Chloe much either. Never hovered and anytime he asked about Tina, Chloe either dodged the question or fed him a line of bullshit.*

The lights were out too, and Merrotti was waiting in the living room the same way she was waiting for Gwen in Hong Kong, in the shadows. If the lights weren't off, then more than likely she would've gazed the detective and turned him into a statue.

"Who's there?" she asked as she searched for the stranger's eyes.

"Relax, Chloe," Merrotti said from the tottering shadows. "Do you know how long it took me to find you?"

"Who are you?"

"I'm the Ghost of Christmas Past."

Chloe didn't recognize the voice or the silhouette. The voice came from a man, obviously. There was pain crinkling inside his voice, which was similar to the pain she had heard from her father. But she had buried him years ago.

Chloe made her last warning: "If I flip on this light switch behind me, I must warn you that what happens next will have detrimental side effects on your health."

"I'm not your enemy, Chloe."

"Then, who are you?"

Merrotti leaned forward and revealed his scarred face in the beam of moonlight.

"An old friend," he said.

"I have no friends."

She didn't recognize the face. It was too disfigured. Then, after she studied him closer, she realized the man had no face.)

Mark asked, "What did he want from you?"

Chloe followed, "He wanted to give me a way back."

(*They skipped the introductions.*

Chloe stood next to Merrotti in front of the moonlit window.

The scars were so bad on his face that she had a hard time looking at him.

So, she kept her eyes on the moon.

"This is my life, Detective," Chloe said, tracing her eyes across the moonlit land outside the window.

"How much longer can you pretend to be someone you're not?" Merrotti said fiercely. "I've seen what these people are capable of. If I can find you, then they can. And they will, Chloe. They will."

"The game has changed, Detective," she said. "It's not the Company I should be worried about. It's something far worse."

Merrotti replied, "You might be able to keep your head down for another year or maybe two, but then what? What will you do when that time comes?"

"I'll do what I've always done, Detective: survive.")

"How did he convince you?" Mark asked.

(*Before Merrotti left, he placed a folder on the desk.*

"We need you, Chloe," he said as he cracked open the front door. "I need you."

Merrotti exited while Chloe walked to the desk and flipped on the lamp. She didn't want to see the contents of the folder; and yet, in the back of her mind, she knew she had to. A corner of a photograph was left exposed outside the edge of the folder. The corner showed a young girl's arm, or what appeared to be a young girl's arm. It was phallic-shaped. And that was all it took for Chloe to open the folder. Chloe knew that whatever remained in that folder wasn't going to be good. It was going to be bad, very, very bad. But she had to see.

She opened the folder and found many photographs of young girls. Some of them were bound or gagged while others were as bare as the day they were born. The detective even took photographs of Louis's entire setup. He had expanded over the years, Louis had. His tastes had evolved too. He had strange devices, all homemade, in the dungeon where he lured his prey. The detective also had photos of Louis, all, of course, taken from a safe distance. It was as if the fucker hadn't aged a year. He was still thin too.)

Eventually, after some thought, Chloe answered, "Devon deliberately left those pictures behind because he knew they would get me back into the game."

"So, he used them as leverage?"

(After Chloe looked through all of the photos, she was so disgusted that she burned them in the fireplace.)

"That's one way of putting it," she said. "Another would be that he needed a new partner in crime."

"And how did you feel about that, having someone working by your side?"

"Good," she said. "It felt good."

"Why?" Mark asked.

Chloe replied, "For so long, I had been doing this on my own. It was good to have someone in my corner for once."

(Chloe arrived at the hotel address that Merrotti had given her before he left the ranch.

She knocked on the door.

There was a soft thud from where Merrotti had placed his gat on the table before he cracked open the door.

Half of his face was concealed behind the door. The other half was masked by the darkness of the room.

"All right," Chloe said to Merrotti. "I'm in.")

Chloe gave Mark the lowdown on Louis Bringer: "He (Louis Bringer) was using his ex wife who worked at Child Protection to cover up his tracks. She'd lure the girls into Louis's custody, and then I don't have to explain what he did next."

"Why now?" Mark asked Chloe. "You had other chances to confront Louis Bringer. Why did you choose to do it with Mr. Merrotti?"

"I wasn't ready after I left Louisiana," she said. "Somewhere in the back of my mind, I was hoping that Louis had changed, that he had a family, that he had a new life, new life, and all that shit he had done in the past was no longer a part of his life. *But* once Devon came to me with those pictures, I realized that... some people don't change. The damage was already done. He made his choice."

"And what choice was that?"

(*They were parked two houses down from Louis's house, Devon behind the wheel, Chloe in the passenger seat.*)

"He was still living in Mississippi, but he was going by a different name."

"Which was?"

"Chris Curthy."

(*Merrotti spotted Louis Bringer's brown Pinto turning onto the neighborhood street.*

"There he (Chris Curthy) is," Merrotti said as he pulled out the pistol from his holster.

He checked the round in the chamber.

Chloe looked at the pistol.

"That's not necessary."

Seconds later, two vans pulled up behind Louis's Pinto.

Four men stepped out of one van.

Three in another. One was burly.

Chloe asked, "What the hell is this?"

"Looks like a party to me."

She clenched her teeth.

"On second thought, bring the gun," she said. "Just in case.")

Chloe: "There was an entire underground group of these—I'd say men, but once a man crosses that line in the sand, he can no longer be considered a human being anymore. And that's exactly what they were, dead men; they were in the shell of a man, but they *weren't* men; they were monsters." She scowled, just barely, just enough to be acknowledged by whoever or whatever waited behind the mirror on the wall. "And like all monsters," she said, "good or bad, they have to answer to somebody."

(*Merrotti took the rear.*

Chloe, the front.

One of them—the burly one—was guarding the base-ment door.

Behind that door, she knew, was where Louis held his business—in the basement.

Chloe took him out!

No biggie.

She never killed him, though, only left him paralyzed from the waist down.)

"There were so many girls down there—eleven of them," she said to Mark. "Some curled in the corner like a bunch of frightened animals. They were dirty and malnourished. They looked as if they hadn't eaten in days."

"How old were these girls?"

"Some of them were in their mid to late teens. Oth-ers. . ."

(Chloe sneaked her way into the basement without be-ing detected.

The sound of girls screaming and moaning drowned out her footsteps.

One of the girls was going down on another man while another one was watching as he played with himself.

There were more girls in the basement; however, they were in a more secluded room.

As she made her way across blind corners, she heard a girl shrieking, now in horror, from behind the door. Then, the slapping, she heard. The slaps were loud too—each one louder than the previous one.

Chloe searched around the basement, looking for some-thing to use to kill the man. Something sharp, Chloe told herself, something that would make him remember. . .)

". . . not even older than twelve years old."

"How did it feel?" Mark asked.

(A couple of gunshots rang out!

Merrotti never killed them.

Neither did Chloe.

Instead, Merrotti took away their weapons, both of them. He took out their kneecaps first, so they couldn't scurry away back to whatever hole they dwelled in. One of them had drawn a pistol on the detective. Merrotti shot him in the hand. Then, he shot him in the other one. So, he wouldn't be able to draw a pistol ever again.

Next, Merrotti shot one in the groin. Then, he took out his weapons. Both of them. He never killed them, though.)

"It happened so quickly." She remembered the blank expressions on their faces. Never will Chloe forget those looks. "We were good. We were quick. We were like ghosts, and it was like we'd been haunting for years. After they were incapacitated, Merrotti tipped off the police."

(*From a distance, they both sat in the parked car and watched police officers rush into the house.*

The police came across one guy in the basement who had the worst injuries. Half of his face was shattered. His right eye socket was shattered. All of his teeth broken. Chloe had found a rusty pipe propped on the wall. It wasn't sharp, but it was just blunt enough to get the job done. She beat the pervert senseless, leaving the right side of his face beyond recognition. If Merrotti hadn't come in there sooner and pulled Chloe from the perv, she would've beaten him to death. No question about it. Chloe wanted to leave no sign that she was there. So, Chloe never fully gazed the other men. Just enough to keep them immobile.

Several minutes after the police stormed the house, a couple of officers carried the frightened girls from the house, each and every one wrapped in blankets—away from harm now, away from the monsters.

Merrotti turned to Chloe, who was seated in the passenger seat.

"*Now,*" he said as his eyes rolled to the backseat, "*what do we do about him?*")

"We found out later that they were tried in court," she said to Mark. "Four of them were known felons. One was a family man. Even had a girl of his own. They all went to jail for life."

"Why didn't you kill them?"

"I wanted to so badly." Then, Chloe corrected, "I could've easily killed them. Who wouldn't? But killing them would've been the easy way. In jail, they still have to live with themselves. And that. . . that's more punishment than death. Putting them behind bars was the *right* thing to do."

"What about Louis Bringer?"

(*They stopped at the edge of Lake Citrine, known for its yellowish tint, which locals called Lake Piss.*

Merrotti popped open the trunk.

In the trunk lay Louis Bringer who was bound by the wrists and ankles with zip ties; and he had duct tape over his mouth.

Merrotti grabbed Louis by his feet, dragged him from the car, and tossed him aside.

He nodded at Chloe.

"He's all yours," Merrotti said and walked back to the other end of the car.)

"He didn't even recognize me." She shrugged. "I didn't expect him too. The last time I saw him in person was over a decade ago."

(*They both shared a long stare, but she never gazed him. Not once. Again, that would be too easy for the both of them, mostly Louis. Chloe walked over to his shrunken body and ripped the duct tape from his mouth.*)

"That face," she said, "that smile, it was the same one I've carried around with me ever since I was a girl."

"Chloe, what exactly did you do to Mr. Bringer?"

(*Chloe looked to her east, through the woods. Above the trees, she saw a cloud of black smoke from a factory.*

She asked Louis, "Do you hear that sound?"

"What the fuck do you want from me?" he whined.)

"What did you do to him, Chloe?"

(*They drove to a sawmill factory, which was located just a mile from the lake.*

Merrotti pulled Louis from the trunk of the car—same way as he did before—and strapped Louis to the conveyer belt, which was used to transport logs through a massive saw. Chloe made sure both of his legs were spread open for the saw; and then, after that, she double checked his genitals and made sure they were lined up correctly.)

"I wanted him to know what it felt like. . . "

(*She switched on the conveyer belt and then the saw next.*

The belt carried Louis toward the massive saw.)

In a trance, she said, "For years, I lived with that pain inside me."

(*His screams pierced the air with horror. He even shitted himself while riding along on the conveyer belt.*

The detective couldn't watch it. Just the sight of what was about to happen was enough to churn his stomach. He wasn't sure whether or not Chloe had the guts to go through with it. Earlier, Chloe told him—with a burst of confidence—that she'd take care of Louis and that she knew what she was doing.)

"At times," Chloe said, "the pain would come and go. But no matter what, it was always there with me."

(*With the saw just inches away from his testicles, Chloe turned off the machine.*

Then, just before Louis passed out from shock, Chloe whispered in his ear, "You're not getting away that easy.")

Mark asked, "How did you feel afterwards?"

(*The Commissioner of the Jackson Police Department, Commissioner Dee Rosenfelt, came across Louis, who was shivering like a wet dog, on the steps outside the precinct. Louis had soiled himself more than once—so much that it was no longer solid. He reeked of something awful too, enough to gag a pig. For days, they had been looking for this "Chris Curthy" fella. Chloe hand delivered him to them, reeking of his own piss and shit.*)

She thought about the question first and then thought about how Louis Bringer had made her feel. Whenever she thought of him, of Louis, she not only thought about

(*those murky eyes, she saw, always blinking them when he didn't speak, and yet it was like he was speaking when, in fact, he wasn't or cracking his jaw, which sounded like a balled-up hand shuffling around old bones or his smile, a creature's smile, as sharp and pointy as a trowel*) but also a running saw—not the sound of it, but the shape of it, as well as its cruel bite.

(*Louis's body, as narrow as a blade, teetered across a dark hallway. There was a faint light from another room behind him, which cast a shadow along the wall.*

With a handful of blankets—hoping they'd keep her safe from the ugly monster—she remained hidden under the bed. Louis's shadow stretched across the walls, now teetering closer to the bedroom. Soon, he would come, she realized. And soon, Louis would find her hiding in the same place where she always sought refuge, and when he did find young Chloe, he would bring nothing but pain.)

She finally said, "I felt nothing."

"You felt nothing?" Mark said. "Would you have felt better if you had killed Louis Bringer?"

"No," Chloe replied. "He was where he belonged, although I knew in the back of my mind that those poor girls would never, I mean, never forget what happened to them. That face would be forever seared in their memories."

"What did you do after Louis Bringer was locked away?"

"There were still more of them out there, ones like Louis. First, we went after the ex. She had changed her name too. She was going by the name of Patricia Forger."

(*Merrotti removed the black bag from Patricia's head, causing her to let out a sudden grunt. Her bloodshot eyes swam around her head and tried to gather the bleak surroundings of the gutted barn. Her eyes suddenly honed in on a tall woman, as confident as a model. That woman was Chloe, and she was strutting from the shadows.*

In her hand she carried a long rusty rod with glowing orange letters at the very end of it.

She showed the letters to a terrified Patricia.

The lettering read, "MONSTER."

She said to her, "Amazing what you can buy on the Internet."

As Merrotti held Patricia's hair back, Chloe pressed the scolding lettering against her forehead.)

"I thought about a tattoo," Chloe said. "That's already been done before. But a scar," she grinned, "that's something you can never get rid of."

(They cut in front of a white van, no windows.

Inside was a nine-year-old girl named Eve. She was gagged and bound in the back seat.

Merrotti yanked the man from the seat and broke his leg first, of course, so that he couldn't scurry away.)

"We found the rest of them. People you'd never think of. Everyday people. Normal people."

(Chloe sneaked up on a father who seemed normal. He was the coach for a high school wrestling team. She caught the coach while he was walking a young teenager to his car, which was parked behind a 24/7 store.)

"We made each other stronger, Devon and I. There was no escaping us. There was no escaping our wrath."

(Coach Bruno tried to run.

Merrotti wouldn't let him.)

"Some of them were right there, hiding in plain sight," she said. "The media was calling us vigilantes, but we were only doing what was necessary." Chloe callously shrugged. "After all, the police weren't catching these individuals."

"Why these sorts of people?" Mark asked.

(She pressed her hand against Sally's. Her hand so tiny against Chloe's palm.

They both smiled and laughed.

She removed her hand from Sally's and pointed at a blank spot on her chest.

Sally fell for the trick and looked at the "spot."

Then, Chloe flipped Sally's chin, causing her to giggle.

Chloe laughed too.

Hadn't laughed so hard in years.)

"*Innocence,*" Chloe said to Mark, "it's the most precious gift that humanity has ever been given. It's ours the moment we enter this world, and it's that innocence that helps us grow as human beings. And it can be taken away at any second. When it's taken away, there's no getting it back. It's gone. . . "

(*Chloe held Sally's dead body in her arms.*

There were piles of trash all around her.)

". . . Forever. I knew I was doing it for the greater good."

"How about Mr. Merrotti?" Mark asked.

Chloe said, "Devon wasn't doing it out of the goodness of his heart. I knew he was doing it for another reason."

"What reason was that?"

"At the time, I didn't know. But soon, I would."

"While you and Mr. Merrotti were going after these certain individuals, did you ever fear Mr. Rake would find you?"

"Not until we went after Mathew Doherty. I slipped up. I did the one thing I tried to avoid while Devon and I were on our little. . . crusade. I accidentally let the gaze loose. When the cops found Doherty. . . "

(*Merrotti kicked down a door.*

Chloe was right there behind him. She found the perp sitting in front of a computer, beating off to child pornography. He was going to town too, as if he was about to rip the thing from his groin.

First, she saw what he was doing to himself—obviously.

Then, she saw the hundreds of nude photographs on the computer screen. She knew that face, the mortified expression on it.

How could she ever forget that face?)

"Over time, I grew to hate that face. Never did I want to see that face ever again. Not on any person, boy or girl."

(*All she knew now of the face had been left in pieces of glass over an empty vanity.*

There were more explicit photographs of young girls, she saw, all without clothes. Most, if not all of them, were taken from the basement. Then, something came over Chloe. . . something wicked. She turned his ass to stone— literally. Every other part of Doherty's body was okay, except for his ass, of course, and everything in the vicinity of it, including his genitals as well as the hand that had been tightly coiled around them.)

She said to Mark, "They found the child pornography on his computer and later concluded that the pictures came from Louis Bringer's house. The media made a whole big deal out of it, the discovery of Doherty's body. After that, I knew they would find me. It was only a matter of time."

"You mean the Company?"

"Worse," she said.

"Mr. Rake?"

(*In that second she had a chance to gaze the driver and she did. What she saw was a man who had carried the image of her father, his body standing behind a wall of flames, and then her father killing Rake's father right in front of him.*)

"Yeah," she said despairingly. "Rake."

— 1 1 . 1 9 . 2 0 4 8 —

CHLOE didn't sleep that night.

Not a damn wink.

She lay on the bed and stared at the ceiling until the guard opened the cell door and escorted her to the white room.

—

THEY cut the cataloging short today.

While Chloe was informing Mark about the remaining five suspects involved in the underage sex ring, she became violently ill and was forced to end the session.

— 1 1 . 2 0 . 2 0 4 8 —

"I made a deal with Devon," she said to Mark, "I told him that if he helped me catch this Rake guy, then, in return, I'd help him find Diego."

"And did Mr. Merrotti agree to your deal?"

"The way I looked at it," Chloe said as she leaned back in her chair, "he had no other choice. At this point, there was no turning back. The both of us were neck-deep in this thing."

"Did you two have any particular plan in mind for catching Mr. Rake?"

"No plan."

Chloe sipped from her coffee, quietly.

"We didn't have to waste our energy trying to find him."

"Why's that?"

"Eventually," Chloe said, "he would find us. And he did."

"So, Mr. Merrotti used you as bait?"

She took another sip of coffee and grimaced slightly from its boldness.

Finally: "I guess you can say that. We drove back to Helena. I went back to my life, worked as a waitress at the same diner, while Devon kept an eye out. We expected to be outnumbered. No doubt. So, Devon brought in some extra firepower."

(*"Pleasure doing business with you," Merrotti said as he shook the General's hand.*

That was what they called him, the General. He wasn't actually in the military. Never served a day in his life. Not even a waking hour. However, when it came to firepower, firearms, and ammunition, the General was the go-to guy.)

"Sure enough," Chloe said, "they found us. This time, they came prepared. I suppose Rake learned a thing or two during his time spent working with JeneCorp."

(*It was a quiet Saturday afternoon.*

The diner, The Night-N-Gale, which sat at the edge of a strip mall, was dying down from the lunch rush.

Chloe was finishing her shift.

At the opposite end of the strip mall, a man dressed in black eased the sniper rifle against the ledge of the roof. He was wearing a visor over the top half of his face— nothing like Chloe had ever seen before, nothing like what the Company wore. She remembered Diego wearing one, a visor. She also remembered Diego telling her that the Company had, in fact, given it to him as a token of appreciation. But these were different, modified, she ciation. But these were different, modified, she would later discover.

As Chloe was about to cross the intersection, the sniper adjusted the scope and took aim.

Suddenly, a navy blue Oldsmobile pulled in front of Chloe as she was crossing the street!

It was Merrotti.

"Get in!" he shouted out. "They're here! Get in!"

As Chloe made her way around the car, a couple of gun-shots rang out from above. The shots weren't suppressed. Yet, they were loud and thunderous.

The bullets caught the windows of the car, shattering the glass but missing its target.

Merrotti sped from the intersection while three black Tahoes appeared from behind.

"Fuck," he seethed. "We got company. . . "

Chloe checked the rear view mirror and saw the SUVs closing in.

"Nothing we can't handle," she said to Merrotti.)

"I remember taking out one of them."

(Chloe grabbed an assault rifle from the backseat and shot out the back window as she unloaded the assault rifle on one of the SUVs. A bullet clipped the front right tire, causing the SUV to swerve out of control. It rammed into the backside of a car and flipped in the air. When it landed, it took out two other cars in its path.)

"Then, everything after that was a blur."

(There was a deafening screech from over her shoulder! Merrotti suddenly cried out, "Hold on!")

"Devon was screaming, but I couldn't remember what."

(As Rake and two other men dressed in black dragged Chloe, who had a gash on her forehead—she was uncon-scious as well—from the bloody wreckage, Merrotti finally came to.

There was smoke all around him, shattered glass and debris everywhere he turned. One side of his scarred face was decorated with tiny fragments of glass. None of the cuts were serious, except for the one above his left eye. The cut needed a few stitches, but that wasn't an issue for the detective. It was the blood. The blood was running into his eye, leaving him blinded.

He blindly reached around the headrest and grabbed the assault rifle which was on the roof of the overturned car.

Slapped in a new magazine.

Still blinded in one eye, Merrotti crawled his way from the open window of the driver's side as they carried Chloe to the other car.

"Chloe!" he screamed.

He tried to stand to his feet, but he couldn't from the twisted ankle. He tripped over the scattered debris and tried to stand once more, this time using the barrel of the rifle to prop his body upright. He did for a moment, limping as he fired at the idled SUV just feet away. Then, he was forced back to the street pavement.

On the ground, Merrotti concentrated by squinting his bloody left eye and then aiming for the tires. If he took out the tires, the detective knew, then that would buy him enough time to regain his composure and then steal a car, then chase after them. He fired the rifle, but it was already too late. They had already driven off. However, the detective saw the tags. If they were smart, the SUV was a rental or even stolen. . . If they were smart. But it was worth a shot. Right now, it was all Merrotti had to work with.)

"I remember the darkness everywhere I turned."

(In the backseat, a man placed a black bag over her head as Chloe kicked and squirmed around.)

"The darkness had become me. . . "

Chloe thought about the darkness. . . her darkness. The only thing that lived or breathed in this eternal darkness was pain, a pain so deep, so bright that it throbbed inside the marrow of her bones; and she had a right to call the darkness her own because it had become everything she knew, the darkness, her darkness. Scores of strange hands touched her in the darkness. At times, a light penetrated the darkness and revealed the aquatic hands of bottom dwellers: pincers, whiskers, fins, and assholes. At

At times, metallic hands. At times, the hands looked like hands but were *not* hands. They prodded at different areas of her body, her most tender areas, the sore areas. There were even hands with fingers as tiny as toothpicks.

(*One of the men stuck bamboo shoots underneath her nails.*)

Each poke sent waves of pain throughout both hands as well as her entire body.

If he hadn't come from the fire, then Rake's men would've turned her flesh inside out.

But they didn't.

The darkness was one mean bitch with one helluva bite, but it was hers and hers alone.

She destroyed all thoughts she had of Jon Rake and then she thought of the one person—the only person—who frequently visited her in the darkness. He was there, *Devon*, she thought, to help ease the pain. He came to her and brought the fire, the flames dancing from side to side like cobras for a snake charmer inside the fireplace. Merrotti's scarred, colorless body was next to the fire— partially nude.

With a stroke of her hand, she wiped the scars from his body and then his face; and she saw him for who he truly was. Chloe asked him if they hurt, the scars. He lowered his head, his hand sliding over her wrist, and told her, "*Not anymore.*"

"When I came to, I didn't know where I was," she said.

(*Seated in a flimsy rusty chair, Chloe snapped from her unconsciousness from the reverberating squeak of a hatch door opening.*)

Chloe said mindfully, "The door, I remember. . . the sound of it opening. That sound reminded me of the time we left Cape Town. We escaped on a cargo vessel. The door, it was similar to the one I heard on the cargo vessel."

(*The door was heavy too, as if it took a bit of muscle to open it. She looked around her surroundings, but all she saw was darkness.*)

"How many days did Mr. Rake torture you?"

(*A man removed the black bag from Chloe's head and squatted in front of her body. Her weak eyes adjusted to the hazy light. His face was blurry at first, but after a couple of seconds, his face became clear. He was as courageous as a tiger too. The man squatting in front of Chloe without a visor was Jon Rake, but most who feared him knew him as just Rake, like the garden tool. He was rather short for a man, less than six feet tall. He had a crew cut with a receding hairline. He had a mustache too, pencil thin. He didn't say much to Chloe. The only thing she could make out were those four words: eye for an eye.*)

"Three days," Chloe answered. "They made sure to keep me hydrated. That way I didn't pass out. I remember every second, every minute, every hour of those three days. . . I remember the darkness. . . "

"Being the last of the bloodline at the time, why do you think Mr. Rake didn't kill you?"

"He wanted me to feel the same pain he felt over all those years. He wanted me to watch." Chloe hung her head, but only for a moment. "For all I know, Rake would've kept me there in that ship for months. . . years. Little did I know that he was actually trying to save the world, *not* destroy it. Two birds. One stone, I guess. Then, on the fourth day, he found me."

(*A loud thud woke Chloe from her semi-conscious state. She struggled to raise her head from the noise.*

Following the thud, she heard gunshots, screams, death.

A fire broke out across the bridge and spread throughout the entire ship.

One of Rake's men swung open the door to the torture cell and tried to take Chloe away, but a gunshot stopped him in his place.)

"He came through the fire," she said.

(*The dead man fell from her path, revealing him, Merrotti, walking through the fire. However, Merrotti wasn't the first face she saw. It was her father's. In that moment, as brief as it was, Chloe saw her father cruising through the fire.*)

"How did Mr. Merrotti find you?"

"He told me the same way a dog finds his way back home. It was cheesy, I know." Chloe grinned, briefly. "But right then, I knew how much Devon cared about me. He would risk his own life and go through an army to rescue me. I remember his eyes (*the fire*, she saw, *the passion burning inside them*—her father had once shared those same eyes).

(*Merrotti freed Chloe from her restraints, and they embraced one another—Merrotti smelling her hair, her every scent.*)

"We got Rake before he could escape."

(*Rake spun around from the gunshot and fell from the dock and onto the shore below.*

He crawled through the wet sand, both Merrotti and Chloe stalking him.)

"Never have I seen a person carry so much hate for another man other than myself. In some strange way or another, I *knew* Rake. I *knew* the hate that drove him."

"The same hate you carried for Mr. Bringer?"

"Yeah," Chloe mumbled.

(*Rake found a pier to prop himself up against.*

Both Merrotti and Chloe towered over Rake as he took his last dying breath.

"*After I left JeneCorp, I tried to live a normal life,*" *he explained to them as strings of blood ran from his nostrils and then from his mouth whenever he coughed.* "*The thought of your father wouldn't allow me.*" *His weary eyes trailed up Chloe's body; they settled on her strung-out eyes.* "*I r'member your father came around noon. You know there were other kids there too, and they weren't as fortunate as I was. The ones who did survive were left scarred and traumatized from the massacre. They never recovered from the horror.*"

He visualized Chloe's father, Freeze, looming over his dead father; Freeze's fists were covered in blood.

"*Neither did I.*")

Mark asked, "So, did Mr. Rake have anything to do with you and Mr. Merrotti not going after Diego Tovar?"

"No."

(They were somewhere near Corpus Christi.

They were lounging in front of the fireplace, Chloe's hand gently rubbing the scars on Merrotti's body.)

"He was right under my nose the entire time."

Chloe wiped the tears from her eyes.

"I finally found someone who would die for me."

"Did you love Mr. Merrotti?"

She nodded her head.

"Yes."

"More than Mr. Haggart?"

Chloe sharpened her gaze.

"Don't say his name," she said bitterly.

Behind the mirror, the technician read Chloe's brain patterns on a computer screen.

A sudden spike of the needle. . .

That's the trigger, sir.

A stern-faced man, who was dressed in a well-fitted black suit and black tie to match, folded his arms over his chest.

We'll use it later.

Chloe didn't answer the question.

Mark blinked twice.

"Does that name upset you, Chloe?"

"What do you think?"

"If Mr. Haggart was in this very room right now, is there anything you would like to say to him?"

"As far as I'm concerned, that man is dead to me."

—

WHEN she got back from lunch, Mark didn't waste time jumping right into the first question.

"First," Mark said, "did you honestly think you and Mr. Merrotti could settle down and live a meaningful life together?"

The color rose a little in Chloe's cheeks.

"Yes."

"So, you thought it was over? No more running?"

"Yes."

(*They were somewhere outside the city of Monterrey, Mexico.*

"Let's end this once and for all," Chloe said to Merrotti as they sat on an old, weathered porch overlooking the Cerro de la Silla. The sun was hovering just above the saddle-shaped mountain.

Merrotti didn't respond to the remark.

Instead, he stood up from the wooden glider and walked to the railing and let out a sigh, one that was loud and heavy.

"Devon?" Chloe said. "Is something wrong?"

He turned his shoulder and faced Chloe.

He had a look on his face.

Chloe didn't understand the look, not at first.)

"For so long," she said to Mark, "death had become easy for me. It was living that was the hard part."

"What about the deal?"

(*"Your anger does not define you," Merrotti said as he held her by the hand. "It's time for you to let it go from your life."*

"I can't," she cried.

"You can't take on the entire world by yourself," he said to Chloe. "Let it go. . . "

"I can't!")

"When we first made the deal, we had absolutely nothing to lose. When you fall in love, you have *everything* to lose."

"Then, why did you leave Mr. Merrotti?"

Chloe didn't answer the question.

"If you loved him so much, why did you go back to Whisperfront?"

(*Chloe threw as many clothes as she could fit into her duffle bag.*

"Why are you doing this?" Merrotti asked as he tried to stop Chloe from packing.

Eventually, she stopped and finally said, "I need to remember."

"Remember what?" he asked. "He's dead, Chloe."

"I don't give a shit about him."

"Then, what is it?"

"Forget it. . . "

Chloe pushed Merrotti aside and stormed away.)

"Chloe?"

(Chloe parked the car outside the gate of Leatherby Manor.)

Mark asked Chloe, "What were you trying to accomplish by going back to the one place you tried to bury for so many years?"

(She hopped over the cast iron fence and crept through the woods. It was autumn in Whisperfront—around the same time she last left the small coastal town. The trees were mostly stripped of their leaves. It was chilly too, unlike Mexico, which seemed like a strange land compared to Whisperfront, a place that only carried change—as seen in its natural surroundings—as well as death.

It was good to be back.

After wandering for miles throughout the woods, she finally found it—it, being a boulder the shape of an eggshell. It was still the same size and all, although it did look much smaller than it did when she was a child. This was where she and the young man used to meet whenever Chloe managed to sneak away from Leatherby Manor. He was four years older than Chloe, but in adolescence, four years seemed like double. It just happened that he lived with his stepmother on the south side of Whisperfront called the Hollows. One sunny afternoon, he met Chloe at a town fair while he was shooting a water gun at a target. He missed the target and accidentally hit Chloe while she was chewing from a cone of pink cotton candy. A happy accident, it was. He got her hair all wet and ruined the cotton candy too. From there, he and Chloe were as tight as double-knotted shoelaces. They did everything together, however, without the consent of their parent(s). If it wasn't for the young man—not Diego or her father—Chloe never would've had the courage to run away from Whisperfront. And that was exactly what the young man had given Chloe during her state of mourning for her mother and little brother, not only courage, but also friendship, honesty, and most importantly, love.

She found a jagged nose in the shape of a beak on the side of the boulder and took three long strides to its north.

On the last stride, she stopped and kneeled down to the earth.

She cleared away the dead, crispy leaves from the ground until she found dirt. Where there was dirt, there was a chance. She used her fingers and dug through the loose soil. About a foot down into the earth, her fingers struck a solid object.

As she did with the leaves, she cleared away the dirt by using her palms to brush away the debris.

Chloe pulled out a small wooden chest the size of a lunchbox. The chest, she remembered, belonged to the young man, well, not entirely. He had stolen it from the attic. It actually belonged to his father's father, Grandpa Owen; however, the young man had never met his grandfather, only heard stories of him and his travels.

After the hole was cleared, she pulled out the chest and opened it.

"When I was a girl," she told Mark, "I used to hang out with this older boy all the time. His name was Dune."

"Dune? Interesting name."

"His real name was Jesse, but I called him Dune because he had big shoulders with knots on his back. I thought they looked like dunes. So," Chloe sighed, "I called him Dune. We had become good friends. The fist time I came back to Whisperfront after all those. . . those years of living a lie, Dune was nothing more than an abandoned memory. I was so focused on finding closure with my father that I completely forgot about him and the pack we made so many years ago.

(Inside were three artifacts. She pulled out each one of them from the chest. She pulled out the first object, which was a figurine of two white doves, both molded together.)

"What was the pack?"

(Young Dune and Chloe were hidden in the cool shadow of the boulder, which they had called the "dinosaur egg."

Dune showed Chloe the chest that he had stolen from Grandpa Owen.

He asked her, "If you had to bury three objects that would, years from now, be discovered by our children or our children's children, what would they be?"

"The doves," Chloe said to Dune, "to represent friendship.")

"The pack, Chloe?"

(*Chloe pulled out the second object, which was a picture of the two. It was taken at a photo booth at the town fair. Chloe was making a monkey face. Dune, a whiplash face. The sight of the picture caused Chloe to laugh and smile. She remembered Dune putting the picture in the chest to remind them of what the two once looked like when they were kids.*

Next, Chloe reached her hand inside the chest and pulled out the final object, which was scattered across the bottom of the chest. She removed her balled hand from the chest and opened her hand, revealing a palm full of old apple seeds.)

"We made a pack to never grow old like our parents."

The tears ran down her face; and they burned too, when they kept running down Chloe's face.

"Even though. . . Devon was much older than me, he made me. . . he showed me what it was like to *feel* again."

"Did visiting Whisperfront help you remember what it was like to feel?"

"Yes."

"To love?"

"Yes."

"So, you were in love with Mr. Merrotti?"

(*Outside Monterrey, Merrotti said gracias to the local bartender and left the bar. He wasn't drunk. Not his style. Not anymore. It wasn't like his days as a functioning alcoholic, or even like the darker days when he binged. He learned a little thing called moderation. Picked it up from Chloe. He only had two cervezas. Just enough to take off the edge. But it was that edge that Merrotti needed once he stepped out of the bar.*

Before he knew what had hit him, he stumbled forward from a sudden blow to the back of his head.)

Chloe wiped away the tears. She pinched her nose, hoping to prevent the phlegm from draining down her nose.

"I told you," she said angrily. "Don't you listen?"

(On the drive back to Monterrey, Chloe couldn't stop smiling.

Miles and miles of paved road and then a dirt road, showing her the way back home.)

"How did you feel when you arrived in Monterrey?"

"Glad," she said over a tense silence. "I felt glad to be back."

(Chloe parked along a side road.

They were scheduled to meet at their favorite café.

Merrotti was nowhere around.)

"Were you ready to settle down with Mr. Merrotti?"

"Yes," she said. "I was."

(Across the café, Merrotti was kicking and screaming in the backseat of a parked black SUV, not a Tahoe like before, but a Suburban with tinted windows. His screams and roars and cries went unnoticed from the gag around his mouth.

Mark asked Chloe, "How did you feel after you realized this man whom you loved so dearly had been captured?"

(A strange suspicion came over Chloe.

She stopped at the edge of the dusty street, gazed one of the locals who had apparently witnessed the whole thing go down.)

"Devon and I always talked about finding a nice quiet spot on an island. Maybe somewhere near the Philippines."

(Chloe's finger traced over a map, which was held down by a salt and pepper shaker, until it came across an exotic island outside Australia.

"New Zealand?" she said jubilantly to Merrotti.

"How about somewhere more exotic?" Merrotti replied, tossing an old baseball in the air.

"More exotic? Huh?"

"I got it." Merrotti caught the old baseball and sat up-right from the lounge chair. "The Philippines," he said to Chloe. "I've heard about this one place. It's called Bora-cay Island. They say the beaches are as white as sugar. The water, so clear you can see the fish.")

"Somewhere they'd never look."

("Boracay Island?" Chloe nodded. "Okay.")

"We figured we'd be safe there, in the Philippines," she said. "There'd be nobody around for miles to bother us."

The thought alone of her and Merrotti lying on a ham-mock together ran across her mind.

"We'd live out our lives," she said in a trance. "We'd die in peace. I knew there was only one ending for us and I chose to ignore it. Maybe in the back of my mind I wanted to let him in because I knew the ending before it even hap-pened."

"Let him in?"

Chloe paused, hung her head.

"My heart."

(There, in the local's mind, she saw Merrotti, gagged and bound by the wrists, being escorted to the black SUV. There were others with him, men in suits.

The Company, Chloe knew.

They found us. . .)

"How did you feel after Mr. Merrotti was captured?"

"I felt empty."

"Why? You didn't feel angry at all?"

"No."

"Why?"

"I knew it was over. I knew there was no way of getting Devon back. The game was over."

(Chloe carefully ducked into a side alleyway as four men disguised in street ware approached her from each angle. She found a motorcycle—what better odds? The keys were in it. Chloe hopped on it and managed to lose the agents. She kept riding. She rode into the night, but she didn't stop. She kept riding until she ran out of gas. Then, she filled up the tank and kept riding.)

"I knew there was a higher power punishing me. I knew that I would *never* find happiness. And even if I ever found happiness, I knew this power, this. . . force, it would be there to stand upon my shoulders and tell me, 'You're *not* supposed to be happy.' I *was* happy with Devon."

"And how did that make you feel, Chloe, knowing that your god—whatever you call it—felt such animosity towards you?"

"Betrayed," she said. "I felt betrayed."

Once more, she cleared the tears from her eyes.

"When I came back home, I felt like He had showed me a path. And I followed it. I followed it every step of the way. I never gave up on wanting to believe. I wanted. . . I wanted to believe in good, but. . . If I knew that path was going to be filled with so much misery and pain and abandonment, so much. . ." she caught her breath, ". . . I would've never walked that path."

Chloe imagined *not* removing the weight from her ankle and descending below into the darkness of the ocean until it was all she knew.

She said, "I would've let the weight carry me into the abyss."

Then, darkness became her.

— 1 1 . 2 1 . 2 0 4 8 —

"DID you sleep any last night?"

Chloe did, a little.

"Nope," she told Mark.

"Are you feeling nervous about tomorrow?"

"A little."

"Just a little?"

"Yeah. . ."

She peered closer into Mark's dead eyes.

"But you already knew that," Chloe said.

She detected a voice in Mark's ear, saying something like *Proceed with the documentation.*

Next: *we have a lot of ground to cover. . .*

Mark repeated, "We have a lot of ground to cover."

She said with a twinkle in her eye, "We do, indeed."

Mark asked, "Now knowing the people responsible for capturing Mr. Merrotti, what was your next step?"

She mostly fiddled around with her hands—peeling hangnails from her fingertips. She drew a drop of blood from one nail, but she cleaned it by sucking on the tip of her finger until the blood was no more. She removed her finger from her mouth and tilted her head in curiosity from the blood's tartness.

Mark waited motionlessly for Chloe to answer.

She finally answered, "There was always a voice in the back of my head telling me that it would work and that I could still live a normal life. There was just a piece of me that *still* believed."

Mark replied, "You could've disappeared for good, Chloe. If you knew there wasn't a chance for Mr. Merrotti, why did you go after him?"

Chloe said flatly, "I just had to know."

"If you really thought you could live a normal life, especially with the power you harnessed, why did you come back?

"I told you."

"Did you want to live a normal life?"

"Yes."

"Then, why did you really come back?"

"Because I *had* to know."

Anger rose in her voice.

"Know what?"

She placed her hands aside.

"I had to know what happened. I needed closure."

(*For hours, she had contemplated using the gaze. She spent most of those hours pacing around the hotel room in Hermosillo.*

She couldn't wait around any longer.

She had to know.

So, Chloe did the one thing she feared the most after she left Hong Kong.

*She found an Internet café on the outskirts of the city—
a dump run mostly by pimple-poppers and fidgety gamers.*

It was closed, but that didn't stop Chloe.

*Once inside, she found a computer, turned it on, and
accessed the Internet.*

Then, she used the gaze.

And used it well too.

To the max.)

"How did it feel?" Mark asked.

"I could feel them crawling underneath my skin."

"Feel who?"

"People," Chloe said vaguely, "millions of them, moving
like tiny currents."

*(Millions of images suddenly scrambled on the screen,
each one violently flashing at a seizure's pace over Chloe's
face.*

*Her eyes absorbed each flash, each image taken from
surveillance videos, web cam videos, cell phone videos, any
electronic device connected to the Internet.)*

"These currents became heavier against my skin,
tighter, like that pin and needles feeling, only excruciat-
ing. And then, it just happened. . . "

Mark asked, "What happened?"

"I don't know," Chloe replied as she shook her head.
"Each thought I had turned into a command. I used facial
recognition systems, satellites; I accessed every surveillance camera in Mexico, every cell. The power," she shook
her head once more, "it was too great. I tried to stop, but I
couldn't. It was like a drug. I wanted it to take away the
pain."

"And did it?"

"Yes," Chloe said quietly. "I wanted it to take me
deeper. It did. I wanted it to erase all memories I had of
Lansford, Whisperfront," her voice trembling with misery,
"of my father until all I remembered was Devon. So, I let
it. I didn't stop searching until I found him."

*(Chloe used the grid—each light was like a star in a
moonless sky.*

She found the one light, her light.

It led her to an island south of America.

That island was Cuba.

Then, the signal stopped at Guantánamo Bay.)

"What exactly were you planning on doing when you arrived at Guantánamo Bay?"

"I just wanted it to be over with."

(*It was pouring rain when Chloe arrived at Guantánamo Bay.*

She crept through the bushes, a bright light guiding her along the way.

That light was not her light—Merrotti—but a spotlight coming from a detention camp, which was located within a U.S. naval base. The camp was called Camp Delta.

In 2009, President Shaw created an act that would shut down the camp for good and release the detainees to other facilities; however, Congress did not approve the act. . .

The President tried again in 2011, and it passed.)

"Why didn't you avenge the murder of Mr. Merrotti?"

(*In the watchtower, an agent of JeneCorp—Agent Balstar was his name—removed the binoculars from his covered face and said over the walkie-talkie, "She's here."*

As Chloe cowered behind the bushes—planning or not planning her the next attack—she saw a group of heavily armed agents escorting a fragile man from the camp.

His face was concealed with a white bag.)

"It would never end, the running, the chasing, the killing."

Chloe imagined a life on the run, barely escaping with her life, dodging bullets, sleeping with one eye open, constantly looking over her shoulder, and then the killing—and she had to kill, for it was the only way to survive.

Moving meant living.

And living meant killing.

"It would never end," she said.

(*Two agents pushed the fragile man onto his knees.*

An agent removed the white bag from the man's head, revealing Merrotti's bruised face.)

"There is no justice for what we do. There *never* will be. We *don't* deserve to live normal lives. We *don't* own that privilege."

Mark clarified once more, "But you did want to live a decent life, a normal life? No more running."

"Of course, I did. I could've destroyed that entire fucking place if I wanted to. After that, then what?" More anger in her voice, and it raised quickly, so did the needle behind the mirror. "You people would send others after me. It would never end. Yet, the running, the chasing, the killing, it would all repeat itself over and over like a vicious cycle." She tried to calm herself by taking a deep breath. She tried. But the anger was still there, bubbling like a pot of boiling water. When she was hot, she was really hot. When she was cold, she was really cold. Chloe was death. She finally found an in-between and said to Mark, "The only way to end the cycle would be for me to kill each and every person involved, and that meant loved ones, sons and daughters, friends. Then, after that, nobody would have an obligation to seek revenge. Then, it would be over. But doing all of that certainly wouldn't bring Devon back from the grave. Would it?"

(*"You've made your choice," a masked agent shouted over the intercom.*

She remained behind the bushes, not moving, not doing much of anything at all, just watching and waiting.

"Then so be it," the masked agent said and passed the intercom to another agent.

He aimed the barrel at Merrotti's head and pulled the trigger.

Merrotti's head suddenly jerked to the right and then his lifeless body flopped to the ground.

Meanwhile, Chloe didn't move an inch—her hand tightly pressed against her mouth in horror. She didn't gaze either. Maybe that was what they wanted her to do. She didn't do anything, not because she was a coward or afraid, but because this was what Devon wanted her to do.

He once told Chloe that if he ever got caught, "Don't come after me."

Chloe broke her promise, at least half of it.)

The door opened.

A security guard entered the white room.

There was a voice in Mark's ear, but she couldn't make out what it said.

She expected the worst, always did whenever there was a disturbance.

Mark acknowledged by blinking twice.

The glossy-eyed guard approached Chloe.

Mark said to Chloe, "You have a visitor."

"Visitor?" she said. Chloe felt a sudden blow to her stomach as if someone had given her a nice whack. Her heart rate increased, said the monitors behind the mirror. Chloe cleared her throat and said once more, "What visitor?"

—

SHE was escorted down a narrow hallway, which, like the white room, was a blinding white color, no expression, just as dead as Mark, until she arrived at another room.

She had never been in this room before, although it looked similar to the other room where she spent most of her time, the white room. The room was free of furniture, except for the rectangular table with two chairs in the middle of the room—just like the white room. The only difference was that there wasn't a mirror in the room. Everything else was the same.

They sat Chloe down at the table and removed the shackles from her wrists and left the room without saying a word to her.

Seconds later, another door opened at the other end of the room.

Then, a young man stepped into the room.

Chloe suddenly stood from the chair and looked at the young man.

For a moment, Chloe didn't recognize him. *He had grown so much*, she thought. Then, Chloe reminded herself that time had drawn out since then and it certainly hadn't been so forgiving, as she would suspect.

"Aaron?" Chloe said surprisingly.

The young man was eighteen years old. He had wavy dark hair that was neatly combed to one side of his scalp. He had two dots underneath his right eye, not both, like Chloe; however, the two scars were faint and hardly noticeable. He had a thin face, high cheekbones. He looked like Chloe from the nose down and his father from the nose up. He didn't have her eyes; in fact, his eyes were green. He didn't have the power to gaze either. He was just a typical eighteen-year-old with issues—his issues, although quite rare, were issues, nevertheless. He was dressed in an all white suit, no tie (they had done away with ties about a decade ago—the new trend was a collar worn around the neck like a priest's collar).

He stepped forward, revealing pieces of himself.

"Hello, Chloe," he said vacantly.

She furrowed her brows.

Chloe, she wondered, *they've been talking to him.*

But that didn't bother her the least. She was more bothered as to what they were telling her son. Were they trumping her up to be the dangerous serpent she had abandoned so many years ago?

So many years had passed.

To Chloe, that creature was no more.

She ambled toward Aaron and then finally hugged him.

"Did they hurt you?" she said, looking over his body for injuries.

Aaron kept both of his arms down by his side. Not once did he lift them upward to embrace his mother.

"No," he said as Chloe pulled back. "I'm fine."

"How's Nina?"

"Fine."

"That's good."

Chloe looked over her son once more.

"Are you sure they didn't hurt you?"

"Yes," he said louder. "I told you 'I'm fine.'"

She looked into his milky eyes and sighed from the sight of them.

"They don't trust me," she said. "Do they?"

"No," Aaron said bluntly. "I chose to wear them."

Chloe's face slackened.

"Aaron?" Chloe said confusedly. "I'm your mother. Nothing has changed that."

Aaron seethed, "*Everything* has changed."

"What have they been telling you about me?"

He paused.

Then, he answered, "The truth."

"Aaron. . ."

She removed her hands from her son's shoulders. She saw the betrayal in his face—his jaw, now flexing.

"Why?" he said, bitterness in his voice. "Why didn't you tell me?"

"One day," she said, "when the timing was right, I was going to tell you." Closer now. "I'm *so* sorry. Aaron. . ."

Chloe pulled her head away, trying not to cry in front of her son.

Aaron acknowledged the distress in his mother's face and yet he felt nothing for it.

". . . Words can't explain how sorry I am for bringing you into this mess. It was my job to protect you from these people and I failed as a parent. All of this is my fault, *not* yours." Her voice sharpened, her manner too. "Now, you're a man and you have to make decisions on your own. Do you understand?"

Aaron could hardly look his mother in the eyes.

"Aaron," Chloe said to Aaron, "please. . . don't do this. You can't. . . whatever they've said about me, it's not true. These people are manipulating you. Don't you see? And they will do anything and everything in their power to turn you against me, even it means raising you as if you were their own. But they're *not* yours, Aaron. They're *not* your blood. You're *my* blood, and you always will be."

"They may not be my blood, but they've given me something that you *never* gave me. . ."

"Aaron?" she said abruptly. "I only did that because I wanted to be a part of your life as much as you were a part of mine—"

"A part of yours?" Aaron said with frustration. "I don't even know who you are anymore."

"I'm your mother, Aaron," Chloe said as she stepped closer. "That's the truth."

Aaron had nothing else to say to his mother.

A long pause rippled throughout the stale room.

Chloe thought of the time when they were younger—just her and Aaron. He was around eleven or twelve years old and Nina was off doing her own thing with her girl-friends. Unlike Nina, Aaron didn't have a lot of friends. The only true friend he had was his mother. There were two memories that stayed with her the most. The first one was a game she and her son played.

There was one in particular. . .

On the way to the comic book store (twice a week she would drive her son to the store, Hero's Hangout, off Main Street, and buy him two comics of his liking), they played the game, Punch Buggy.

She would always be the first one to spot a bug—a Volkswagen Beetle.

(*"Punch Buggy!" she yelled out and punched Aaron in the arm.*

Chloe never punched him hard enough to leave a bruise.

Just enough to give him a startle and then a laugh.)

The second one: warts.

Not something a person would want to remember some-body by. It was true, though. Chloe remembered Aaron used to get warts on his fingers all the time. She called him Toady. There was another nickname Chloe had for Aaron, one she used more than Toady, and that name was Binky.

(*I want my binky,* Aaron would say as a child, referring to his blanket.)

So, Chloe called him Binky.

The nickname ended up sticking the most. Plus, she thought it sounded better than Toady.

"We used to be friends," Chloe said. "Didn't we?

Aaron didn't respond.

"Listen, I know there are things that I kept secret from you," she said. "And I'm sorry for that. I'm *so* sorry. I am. But that's not who I am. *Not* anymore, Aaron. The life that I once lived, it doesn't exist in this place and it certainly didn't exist in Davenport. I left that life behind. I don't have any regrets for what I've done. If I hadn't lived that life, *Aaron*," emphasizing Aaron, "I would've never had such a wonderful son like you." Chloe's manner changed, sharper now, poised. "The only regret I have is not leaving him sooner. The only. . ." Chloe cleared her throat, ". . . the only reason I stayed was because of you and Nina."

Aaron faced his mother, the white tears streaming down his eyes.

"We could've started over, the three of ah—"

"Times I wish things could just go back to the way they were, with you and dad. . . "

"They can't, Aaron—"

"—I know they can't," Aaron cried out, "and they won't. It's too late."

Chloe grabbed her son's hand from below.

He immediately pulled his hand away and took a step back.

"Listen to me, Aaron," she said. "Soon, I will be dead. And that's something you're just going to have to deal with."

The emotion emptied from Aaron's face.

"You're already dead."

"Aaron. . . "

"Don't."

"Aaron. . . "

Chloe took another step forward, but her son took another step back.

"One day, you'll understand," she said, keeping her composure. "Now, I don't expect you to. You have to listen to me when I tell you that I love you, Aaron. I love you *more* than the world itself, and I need you, Aaron, to be strong. Are you listening?"

Aaron hung his head, but Chloe lifted up his chin.

"There's no more time for crying," she said. "Everybody dies. Some of us get chosen sooner than others. That's a part of life. And one day, it will be your time."

Once more, Aaron hung his head, but only for a second. He lifted his head before Chloe had a chance to lift it back up.

"You must never think of death as a sign of weakness or a mark of defeat; but, instead, think of death the same way you think about birth: the beginning of a new life. For now, this is your life. It's *not* their life. It's *not* my life. It's *yours*, and you have to make the best of it before death finds you. Don't listen to what they tell you." She placed her hand over her son's heart. "Listen to your heart. It'll give you light in your darkest hours. It will protect you from your worst enemies. Most importantly, it will guide you toward freedom. When I'm gone, everything is going to change. *I'm* going to change. No matter what you see or what you hear, it will *not* be me. It will be them. Aaron, do you understand me?"

Aaron didn't answer.

"Do you understand?" she asked again.

There was no answer from her son, only a tense glare.

The tears in his red eyes had cleared away some of the solution. Part of the pupil was exposed for the gaze. So, she used it to her advantage. More than likely, this would be the last time she would see her son before the execution.

Chloe accessed the areas in Aaron's brain that processed language, mainly two: the Wernicke's and Broca's area. There, she brought forth one word *there*, and then another, *is*, and finally, the remaining words, *a man who goes by the name, Julius Hampton. He's a writer who lives in Sedona, Arizona. It is important that you go to Sedona and find him.*"

Aaron first thought: *Why?*

I can't explain right now, she gazed Aaron. *When you arrive at the cabin, you'll get further instructions.*

"What cabin?" he asked vacantly.

Suddenly, Aaron snapped from his trance-like state.

"Please, Aaron," she said to him.

With a pallid expression, he looked at his mother—strangely at first and then with incredible fright, not from what she had told him, but from what she had just done to him.

Before she could utter another word, Aaron exited the room.

—

CHLOE couldn't sleep at all.

She tried to close her eyes for a while, but she spent most of the night tossing and turning.

One of the guards was told to give her a drug to help her relax (Chloe didn't exactly know what it was), but it had little to no effect on her.

The night was spent thinking of that one day when she passed through the town of Davenport. She spent a couple of years in both Dakota's—North, the shortest—and then she moved back to Montana; however, that didn't last too long. By now, Chloe had traveled the world, except up North. She never was a cold-weather-kind-of-gal, but she wanted it now more than ever—the cold. If the car wasn't running on E, then Chloe never would've stopped. Chloe would've kept riding with the sun on her back and the Pacific Ocean breeze thickening in the air. Plan A was to stop at a nice little spot called Everson (she saw it once while skimming through a shelf-full of brochures at a highway diner). It sat in the foothills of the Cascade Mountains—the ideal place to hide from the Company. She figured she'd hang out in Everson for a month or so before trekking north into Canada. However, if she hadn't stopped in Davenport, Chloe never would've stumbled into Plan B—*Whatever happens happens*. It all started after she filled up the tank with thirty dollars-worth of gasoline. Chloe paid the kind clerk, and as she was exiting the convenient store, she felt the door recoil; and then she heard a loud thud outside. She hurried outside the store, only to find a poor man on his knees. He was clutching his nose, which was dripping with blood. The blood, she saw, was pooling into his cupped hands. He raised his head upright—a subtle pain still rippling throughout his face—and saw a pretty brunette kneeling downward, something special in her voice. Their eyes crossed paths. It was like the big bang all over again. A warm feeling instantly exploded inside their chests, the shrapnel raining down into their guts. Toby was his name—she would later learn. She witnessed the pain dissolving from his face and then his eyes, both of them brightening like emeralds in the sun. Her eyes brightened too. She went back inside the store, grabbed a couple of towels from the clerk who saw the whole escapade go down, and cleaned the blood from Toby's nose until it finally stopped gushing blood. They talked for a few minutes and yet, after a few minutes, they acted *not* like strangers, but like two pals who had known each other for years. There were no hiccups. No awkward pauses, except for when she stumbled with her name. In Montana, she was Rebecca. In Washington, she was Rebecca. *No!* Bella. No tense moments either, except for when Toby asked Chloe out on a date. Chloe had never met Toby before and vice versa, but for some reason, at that moment, she was glad she had.

Later that day, she decided to hang around Davenport. She piddled around the town until nightfall and got a hotel room on the outskirts of town.

She had spent the past few years mostly to herself. The last time she had been with a man was about a year ago. She was in Reno, Nevada, for a weekend. She found joy in riding in the car with the window down and driving until her back was sore and her legs were ready to fall off. He was older than her, about ten years. The guy was loaded too—had a fancy gold watch and hair plugs and a spray tanned face—which Chloe had used to her advantage. She wasn't looking for love. She was at the very beginning of her cycle—just days past her angry bitch phase—and she was feeling hot, not hot as in feverish, but hot as in she was in the mood for a guiltless fuck in order to clear the cobwebs. And forget about the vibrator. It was running on its last leg. And he had to be old too, Chloe reminded herself before she arrived in Reno—not some horny young buck who was riddled with diseases from doing it bareback every time he stuck *it* in. She got what she wanted, a guiltless fuck—and it was good too, the fuck of the year—as well as the man's wallet; and she left Reno without feeling the least amount of guilt, especially after she learned that the guy was a womanizer.

I needed this, she told herself, but that sneaky demon inside had another motive.

For the longest time, she stared at the name of the restaurant written down on the back of the Pit Stop receipt. It was called Q-Shack; and this man, Toby, had told her that if she was interested in joining him for supper, then he'd be there at the Q—that was what he called it.

No!

Bella!

Fuck it, she said.

When she arrived at the Q, she found him sitting alone at the bar. She got halfway into the restaurant (the point where he had made eye contact with her and she with him). At that moment in time, she saw another person seated with him, in fact, half his size. Next to him sat a young girl, but Chloe was more in-tuned with that intoxicating light in Toby's eyes. She still felt a little bad for what she had done to the man—after all, he looked like Rudolph the Red Nose Reindeer—and she had no obligation to join him for supper. When she got to the bar, Toby introduced her to his daughter, Nina, who was six years old, going on seven. The resemblance to Sally was uncanny—same hair, same eyes, same cute smile; but Chloe was more baffled because he never brought up the kid in the earlier conversation. For some reason, though, Chloe decided to stay. She had supper with both Toby and Nina, and after Nina had fallen asleep, they walked around town, talked, and looked at constellations in the night sky. The only action Chloe received was a goodnight peck on the cheek. Toby invited her to a town parade, which took place the following day. Chloe agreed. *Whatever happens happens.* One day in Davenport turned into two days, two days into a week, a week into a month, two months, six months, nine months, a year; and then a couple of years later, on a crisp summer night (Nina was sleeping over at a girlfriend's house, and Chloe and Toby had the house all to themselves), Chloe got knocked up. Not once did she ever think about having kids, especially with her situation. When she worked as a telemarketer at USR, she thought about having kids. But that time had come and gone. She thought she was way too old to push out a baby. She knew she had a clock when it came to pregnancy, and she was well beyond that time. Thirty-five was a fair deadline for her; but forty, that was gambling with a shit hand. But life wasn't about dealing with a good hand. It was about learning how to deal with a bad one.

They got hitched while Chloe was six months pregnant with Aaron. It was a small ceremony, nothing big or extravagant.

Rewind: Now, she thought about a life without Toby, without Nina or her son, Aaron. Chloe would've kept riding for who knows how long or how far. Her travels never ended in Canada. She kept riding until she couldn't ride anymore. She was bouncing from one island to another— the less people Chloe ran into, the more solitude she experienced.

Before Chloe knew it, she was in a country called Greenland, but there was nothing *green* about it. Whoever the fuck named the country must've been colorblind. They should've called the country Whiteland because that was what it was, nothing but white all around her. Chloe found a cozy cottage away from the white, away from people. Now, Chloe was a lonely old woman who spent her days constantly staring at the noose that she had made for herself.

Eventually, that pretty noose grew lips, as well as a tongue, and learned how to speak; and that croaky voice said to Chloe, *Hello, my old friend. What to cuddle?*

Eventually, the loneliness caught up with Chloe, and she was forced to take her own life.

Death by asphyxiation.

Chloe rose from the bed, gasping at first, and then cleared the sweat from her forehead.

She tried to rest her weary eyes, but the thought of Davenport would not let her.

— 1 1 . 2 2 . 2 0 4 8 —

CHLOE heard Mark's question a second time, but Davenport was still on her mind.

She felt the glossy paper crinkle and crack in her hands as she crumbled the receipt.

A cool sensation rushed through the skin of Chloe's face from where she splashed it with cold water.

Did one last primp of her hair.

The full moon driving her.

Fuck it.

She retraced and then honed her wandering thoughts to many years after she mouthed those two words in that herpes-infested hotel room.

A perfect accident was what they later told her, but she knew it was all a setup, the whole fucking thing, with Nina, using her to pull Chloe's heart strings, and then Toby and his background, as well as his mannerisms, which were similar, if not, identical to Devon's, and then, him displaying the obvious signs that he was spending his wakeful nights reporting to JeneCorp rather than catching Zs. It was not only written in his eyes, but the bags he started to carry underneath. There was one instance when she caught him creeping into the house late at night. He said he was taking a late-night walk. Couldn't sleep was Toby's excuse, but when she gazed him (which was something she swore she'd never do again), she saw nothing. Not a damn thing. It was like his mind was a blackboard and every thought from the time they cut off the light to the time he crept into the house had been erased.   All that remained was the chalk dust of lost memories.   There was even another time when he completely forgot Chloe's name, Bella.

That was another sign that something was wrong.

Then, she retraced her thoughts farther back in time.

Now several hours *before* she mouthed those words.

The jingle of a cowbell. . .

Bam!

Farther.

She removed the nozzle from the car and placed it back into the pump's holster.

There was a man, Chloe saw, sitting in a black car next to the convenient store.

Toby, she saw.

He was wearing shades, though.   They had an incredibly dark tint too them—and if they were windshields, they wouldn't have been street legal.

But he was there, Toby, and he was watching Chloe, waiting for that "exact" moment to step in front of the door.

And *Nina*, a bubbly young girl who carried a smile that could cure cancer, wasn't even his blood.   But the thing that was bugging her the most: Was Nina's love for Chloe *real* or was it all an act?   If it was scripted, Nina could've easily taken home an Oscar for Best Supporting Actress.

The question was asked once more, but Chloe was still in her thoughts.

The very last thing Chloe saw in her mind before she snapped from her thoughts was the day she was apprehended.

(*She was folding clothes when she suddenly felt the house vibrate and then she heard the dishes rattling in the kitchen and the family picture frames shivering like jittery teeth against the fireplace mantle.   It had all the qualities of a tremor; however, it carried sound and she knew right then and there that it wasn't a tremor.*

A creeping sensation came over her as she heard the sound of engines, so many of them roaring and rumbling over the clinking and clanking houseware.

Chloe stopped what she was doing and walked toward the front door. There were hundreds of them, she saw, agents standing outside parked armored cars; they were wearing visors; their weapons were drawn; and they were perfectly circled around the entire house.

An agent she had never seen before, Agent Noble, stepped from the barricade. He was a man, Chloe knew, but he was not a man. He appeared modified but important.

As Chloe approached the strange agent, she saw him, Toby, positioned with the other agents.

He was dressed the same as the agents.

He had a gun too.

He had a visor held down by his side.

And he carried no shame in his eyes, no apologies . . .)

None, Chloe thought, *none whatsoever.*

"I said, 'How did the visitation go yesterday?'"

Chloe sighed.

"Fine," she said.

"Did you finally get some sleep?"

Frustrated, she said, "You've been asking me that question for the past week and I've told you the exact same answer."

"Very well. Let's move on and start with the day you met Mr. Haggart."

"I don't want to talk about it."

Mark said, "I assure you, Chloe, this will be the last section of the cataloging. After we're finished cataloging the time you spent with Mr. Haggart, you're not required to answer any more questions. Is that clear?"

"Whatever."

"I take that as a yes."

"Yeah."

Chloe gazed into Mark's eyes, those lifeless things.

Finally, she saw something in them, something useable.

One of the eyes twitched ever so slightly, as if an eyelash got stuck in the corner of the eye. Chloe knew right then and there that Mark wasn't a *he*. Mark was an *it* created by the Company, and that was enough motivation for her.

"How would you compare the relationship between you and Mr. Merrotti to you and Mr. Haggart?"

Behind the mirror: *Here it comes. . .*

Reading is off the charts. . .

Shut it down. . .

Wait a sec. . .

Chloe didn't answer Mark's question.

"Did you love Mr. Haggart the same way you loved Mr. Merrotti?"

Again, there was no answer.

Strangely blinking, Mark persisted, "Would you rather have a child with Mr. Merrotti or Mr. Haggart?"

No answer.

"If Mr. Merrotti was still alive, what would he think of Mr. Haggart?"

Chloe suddenly rose from the chair and hurdled over the table!

When it came, they were left speechless.

Nobody really saw it coming, but somehow, the thought had always lingered somewhere in those refined, economical minds—wondering how Chloe would actually do it to Mark: Would she be so poetic as to poke out its eyes? After all, the manufactures decided to go with aluminum, not copper, which had a low coefficient of thermal expansion. It wouldn't be hard to do, especially for a woman who, over the years, had been molded into a natural born killer. Or, would Chloe burst out in a heap of rage and use part of the chair to stab Mark beyond restoration? Even worse, would she find a way to break the mirror beside her and use the jagged remains to cut it up like sushi, not because Chloe was one violent bitch, which she was, and Chloe was okay with that, but because she was overly curious to see its inner makings?

And the gaze was out of the question. She was well aware of this too. The dicks in charge made sure that Chloe's Jedi mind tricks would have no value in Mark's synthetic flesh.

It was simple circuitry.

All they had to do was turn off *the switch* and redirect the current elsewhere.

Not in their wildest imagination did they ever think Chloe would do *that*.

It was a clean tear too, as if its head was a cork ready to pop. All the skill required was a twist of its neck and then an upward yank by Chloe.

Then, *pop* goes the weasel!

A pall of smoke exploded from its neck, sparks shooting outward every which way.

With Mark's head held in her hands, Chloe took a second to admire its circuitry and the wires and every component that had made the droid look more human than human. The flesh, she observed, wasn't like her own. She ran her thumb across its rubbery texture.

Scowling, she rotated around toward the mirror, reared her right arm behind her back, and hurled Mark's head through the glass.

A sudden shatter and then a *crash* of glass!

The mirror gave way and revealed a group of suited men who went scurrying underneath desks.

After the glass had rained down, one last remaining fragment of glass fell from the pane like an icicle.

After the glass had settled, the control room was revealed in front of her. It was dark inside. There were two control boards, one board stationed on each level, and men dressed in suits—some shielding their pristine faces, while others gradually lifting their heads from the desks. There were scientists and technicians too, not as skittish, dressed in white lab coats—an operator was standing next to PET scans of a brain, which Chloe soon concluded was *her* brain, *not* Mark's. They had other images of Chloe's brain, including thermal imaging and X-rays.

She knew they had been watching her throughout the entire cataloging, but never did she think they were reading her and her brain activity or diagnosing her every movement and word and emotion or calculating every little thing that made Chloe *Chloe*.

Were they pumping chemicals into the room while she slept?

Or, *the coffee*, she wondered, had they been drugging her this entire time?

A group of guards suddenly rushed into the room!

Chloe took out two of them, no problem.

More rushed inside, leaving her without any room to wiggle. They circled around her. Chloe could only take out one of them before she was quickly knocked to the floor. Chloe hadn't used her skills in quite some time—clearly—and the gaze had been tamed from whatever drug they gave her. Not only that, the energy expended from ripping off Mark's head had left Chloe out of breath and with very little strength.

They pulled out long wands from their holsters and shocked her and beat her until she finally surrendered.

"Watch her fucking head!" yelled one of the two agents who stepped through the broken mirror.

The agent was Agent Noble—a "more enhanced" Agent Noble. The right side of his body, including his arm, most of his hip, as well as his ribcage, had been thoroughly augmented with robotics; however, unlike the prototype, Mark, he didn't have synthetic skin to conceal his inner makings, only a black glove, which ran to an artificial elbow. The right side of his face had been badly scarred, but Chloe had seen worse. He lost his right eye, as well, during the explosion in Santa Ana. Instead of wearing a glass eye—as the doctors had suggested—he wore a black eye patch.

He pushed the guards away from Chloe.

One of the guards kicked Chloe in the ribs.

Agent Noble leaped at the guard, grabbed him by the jugular with his right hand—the robotic one—and then squeezed, almost effortlessly, until the guard blacked out.

Another agent stood at the edge of the white room.

The agent's name was Stefan Prescott, Noble's protégé. He looked at the head on the floor, still shooting out sparks and a tiny dark cloud of smoke.

"Seventeen million dollars well spent. . . "

Throughout the legs of suited bodies, Chloe peeked into the control room and saw a monitor on the wall displaying a couple of employees hunkered beneath a desk.

Then, she found Mark's head not too far from the employees, near Agent Prescott—its eyes flickering before fading to black.

And then, she saw, the monitor cut to black and then static.

As Chloe pulled her eyes from the monitor, she found another face, a familiar face—her son's. Chloe knew that face, knew the look on it. She had seen the look a lot when Aaron was a tween. She saw the look whenever he broke something or whenever he told her a lie or whenever he did something he wasn't supposed to do.

Once Aaron saw his mother looking at him, her acknowledging that look, he darted from the control room.

Agent Noble kneeled down and attempted—in a kind manner—to brush Chloe's stringy damp hair over her scalp, but she suddenly wrenched backward.

"Hush," he whispered to Chloe, trembling with both fear and anger.

The agent tried again and this time he succeeded.

"I'm sorry you had to see that, Chloe," Agent Noble said as he stroked Chloe's matted hair.

"Just do it already," Chloe said feverishly.

Agent Noble grinned, a wicked thing.

"Soon, Chloe," he said. "Very soon."

The agent held out his left hand—the real one.

Chloe eyed the hand for a second.

"Come," he said.

There was an image in the corner of her eye. She moved her eyes away from his hand and saw another monitor in the secret room. There was a still of two strange men seated inside a car, which was parked next to

a convenient store. One of the men, she saw as she focused on the screen, was Toby. He was wearing black
sunglasses. They had an incredibly dark tint too them—
and if they were windshields, they wouldn't have been
street legal.

"Ah ha," Agent Noble said as he followed Chloe's eyes to
the still behind him. "We call it visual mapping."

Visual what?

"We were able to reverse the gaze and use Mark," he
shot a glance at Mark's headless body, "or what used to be
Mark—to produce a mental projection of what really goes
on in that head of yours. Pretty cool, huh?" There was no
response from Chloe. What could she say to this man?
She was confused and yet furious. Words could never do
justice to how she truly felt. "The difference between
Mark and us, Chloe," Agent Noble said over drawn out silence, "is that Mark will never be able to feel. Mark will
never be able to show any emotions like me or you."

"Shocking," she said sarcastically as the blood dribbled
from the corner of her mouth. "You don't strike me as the
emotional type."

The agent ignored Chloe's remark.

Yet, it stayed with him, marinating.

"Mark will never get angry," the agent said to Chloe.
"Mark will *never* ever get sad. Mark *only* does what it is
told, and we," he traced his tongue over his bottom lip, "we
have the power to take away the one—the *only*—thing
that has led to our ultimate downfall. . . "

Chloe listened carefully, waited.

"*Free will*," Agent Noble said sternly.

Once more, he reached out his hand.

"Come," he said to Chloe.

Finally, she grabbed his hand.

Agent Noble helped Chloe to her feet.

One of the guards grabbed her by the other side.

Together, they escorted Chloe from the white room.

—

THEY took her to the medical bay where they fixed her injuries.

Chloe had two broken ribs and several scrapes and bruises on her arms and legs.

With the proper treatment, as well as advanced medicine, the injuries healed in a matter of minutes; and after she woke from her nap, she was as good as new.

—

CHLOE'S cell door automatically opened.

"Are you ready?" the guard asked.

She stood up from the bed, nodded her head, and released a sigh from her chest, one that had been building ever since she left the medical bay.

She told guard, "Let's get this over with."

And they did.

PART THREE
THE SECOND ASCENSION

THE final days leading up to the *big day* were one big ass blur for Chloe. The Company had gotten what they wanted from her in their state-of-the-art facilities located in Death Valley, except for one last thing, and that had to be achieved in Tokyo, Japan, where they had the proper equipment.

When she arrived in Tokyo—one of JeneCorp's newest facilities (rumor had it that two others had recently sprouted up outside Dubai and then another in Bangladesh)—they didn't waste any time with the process.

There, at Tokyo's high-tech facility, the scientists conducted a series of tests on Chloe, which consisted of basic commands.

The tests ran on for twelve days, Chloe getting very little rest throughout the duration.

Then, after the final tests, they ran last-minute diagnostics on Chloe and made sure there weren't any bugs or glitches or hiccups before the launch of the new operating system.

The last day before the big day was spent in a small room no larger than a closet filled with utter darkness. Why utter darkness? There, they could monitor Chloe's brain activity, as well as her vitals. The sole purpose of the experiment was to replicate not only the mood, *but* also the environment of what it was going to be like for Chloe after the first moments of her execution, or what the Company called behind her back, her "ascension."

When the lights finally flickered on after hours spent in darkness and it came time, Chloe was ready.

110%.

For the past few months prior to the big day, she would have moments of intense anxiety or what doctors called panic attacks. There would be times where it felt as if she couldn't breathe, as if she was ready to leap out of her skin or pass out; the muscles in her chest or throat would tighten like a fist; and the world would start spinning out of control from the lack of oxygen to her brain. The doctor had taught her how to breathe from her gut—*belly breathing*, the doctor called it—and it worked for the time being. The feelings of dread eventually passed, only to return later. Other times, she'd have moments of great euphoria after spending days psyching herself up.

For Chloe, it wasn't the pain that she feared the most, even though they told her that it would be painless. It wasn't the thought of *not* being missed by her loved ones, even though they told Chloe that Aaron would mourn for her when she was gone.

It was the uncertainty of delving headfirst into the unknown.

How terrifying it was, not knowing!

The Company could run as many tests or experiments as they damn well pleased, but when the time came for the real thing, anything could happen.

Chloe knew this.

And for some reason, so did JeneCorp.

—

TWO teams of guards (fitted in different getups from the ones in Death Valley; these were decked out in sleek and all white armored gear with silver lining, as well as combat visors) arrived outside Chloe's holding room. They gave her a white gown to wear, which looked similar to a hospital gown.

They waited outside while she slipped her bare body into the gown; and after Chloe was dressed, they applied shackles to both her ankles, as well as wrists, as a precaution.

Agent Noble escorted her to the operation room at the end of a long and narrow hallway, where she was scheduled for execution.

Like the facility in Death Valley, the walls thrummed with a strange hum. They were brilliant white, expressionless, except for the operation room, which was surrounded by thick panes of glass. Knowing that this would be the last time she would walk again on these two feet was enough to slow down her pace. She did and she *tried* to savor each step, but each step felt as if she was tramping through sand, baby steps. Chloe was careful and mindful of every step, reminiscent. These feet had taken her so many places, through so many memories. Now, she was ready to leave them behind and embrace her new feet. . .

When they made it to the operation room, Chloe found her son pacing around another hallway, which led to the observation room.

There were a couple other people behind Aaron dressed like bureaucrats, none of whom she knew.

Before they entered, Agent Noble said to her, "Are there any last words you would like to say before we begin?"

Chloe directed her attention toward Aaron and said with an expressionless face, "No."

"Very well," the agent said and nodded at the guards.

Agent Noble joined Aaron in the observation room while the team of guards escorted Chloe into the operation room.

The room, she saw, wasn't just any ordinary room.

As soon as Chloe stepped halfway into the cool room, she was aware of the massive scope of the room. It stretched out for what appeared to be miles. There were rows and rows of servers, and they filled the entire hanger. In front of the servers was the operation table.

They escorted her to a strange contraption, which was in the shape of a large metal clasp next to the table. She soon realized that she wasn't going to the table. She was going in that thing, whatever that thing was. Next to this clasp were three server-sized pillars with cables running in and out of them, which fed into a secluded room on the west wing of the room similar to the control room in Death Valley. There was also a conveyer belt-type deal that tracked through the clasp with a glass container directly behind it. The sight of the squared container sent a wave of panic inside her body, starting from her stomach and echoing to her fingertips, which were now numb.

Belly breathe, she remembered.

Two Japanese scientists carefully placed Chloe's head inside the strange contraption.

"You're going to feel a small pinch," the scientist warned her.

They snapped the massive clasp in place and then locked it around Chloe's neck—not tight enough to choke her, but just tight enough to keep her from escaping.

She grimaced from the coldness of the metal against her skin, not the pinch.

"Begin the stimulation," the scientist said expressionlessly to the selected guard.

The guard removed the wand from his belt and gave Chloe a shock.

She suddenly flinched from the shock.

Inside the observation room, Aaron darted toward Agent Noble.

"What are they doing?" he said to Agent Noble.

"Their job."

They continued to "stimulate" Chloe, causing her to grimace. Each grimace grew deeper along her face. She could no longer hold back her screams and then the tears. They came too. And Chloe took it, the pain. Each shock. Not once did she beg or plead them to stop, even though it was right there on the tip of her tongue. Chloe didn't want her son to hear it. However, she wanted her son to *see* it, the pain on her face, the pain in her guttural scream.

Aaron saw it.

And he heard it.

Patiently waiting in the back of the control room were more agents, more bureaucrats, more politicians.

Sitting in a wheelchair was one individual in particular with round dime-sized scars on both of his cheeks. The shadowy man was President William Lockhart; and whenever he spoke, he did so with a soft, crackling voice.

After a recent assassination attempt, which nearly claimed his life, Lockhart hardly showed his face in public and some believed he was, in fact, assassinated and replaced with a look-alike. But these were nothing more than conspiracies. The fact: Lockhart became the kind of man who stayed extremely close to the shadows in order to conceal his power, despite the ambiguous message that his presence or lack thereof sent to the American People.

The technician said to the strange man, "We're almost there. Eighty-three percent."

"Keep going," Lockhart said from the shadows.

The technician replied, "Yes, Mr. President."

They continued to shock Chloe, and her son continued to watch.

He now watched two guards shock his mother again and then again. Then, Aaron saw the pain ripple across her face again and then again. The wrinkles on her face cracked and hardened like the scales of a snake.

Eventually, Aaron could no longer watch.

He suddenly got in the agent's face.

"You lied to me, you son of a bitch!" he snarled, the spit projecting from his mouth.

As Aaron reared his arm back to strike the agent, Agent Noble grabbed his fist with his left hand and strangled him with the right.

Chloe's eyes shot toward her son, who was now dropping to his knees.

She cried out, "Get away from him goddamn it!"

The shocking stopped for a second.

Baffled from the sudden halt, the head scientist watched the number dropping to eighty-two percent on his tablet.

Then, eighty-one, eighty, seventy-nine. . .

"Again!" the scientist demanded.

The guards continued to shock Chloe.

Eighty-one percent. . .

Aaron's face began to turn red, then purple, then blue.

Just before he was about to black out, Agent Noble released the death grip and yelled at the guards standing in the hallway, "Get this ungrateful shit outta here!"

The two guards grabbed Aaron from the floor and carried him away.

"Running diagnostics," said the technician.

Before the guards could remove Chloe's son from the observation room, he broke away from the guards and ran toward the glass.

With both of his hands curled into fists, Aaron pounded them against the glass. He pounded his fist so hard that his knuckles began to bleed, but the sight of the blood didn't stop him. He pounded until his bones broke and then he pounded some more until the glass cracked and chipped.

They both acknowledged one another—Chloe enduring each violent shock and then Aaron finally realizing how wrong he was about JeneCorp.

Ninety-seven percent. . .

Now, six guards grabbed Aaron from behind and dragged him away from the glass as he kicked and screamed.

Then, the execution began. . .

A tiny red laser lit up in the corner of Chloe's eye. At first, she thought it was a floater in her eye or something obstructing her vision, like an eyelash, or even her retina deceiving her into seeing something that wasn't really there.

But it was there, she knew after a second glance.

The red laser was about as thin as a shoelace, blinding at certain angles, and it stretched roughly about nine inches from one mechanism to another.

In the control room, the reading hit a hundred percent.

"It's a lock," the technician said. "We are now synched."

"All right," said Lockhart, "let's do it. We only get one shot at this."

The red laser broke away from the main pillar and ran along a track, which wound around the two other pillars. It rounded the third and final pillar and headed directly toward Chloe.

When it happened, she closed her eyes at the last second. . .

She didn't feel a thing, not even a pinch.

Her entire body flopped to the floor while her neck suddenly squirted blood. Each string of blood randomly sprayed from her neck as if her neck itself was a brush, the finely severed veins were the bristles, and the spotless white floor below was her canvas, and she was paying homage to the great Jackson Pollock; but her head, like an arthritic hand articulating each stroke, still remained intact in the clasp.

An orange fluid was automatically injected into the side of her neck, which was cauterized by a scalding cylinder interface in the shape of a plate.

The scientists made the proper connections to the underside of her stabilized head and then one of them pressed the green button on the control board—green, meaning *go*.

In the control room, the technician said to Lockhart, "Coupling is a success, sir."

Without showing any motion or emotion, Lockhart remained concealed in the shadows.

Then, he said, "Now, stimulate the nervous system."

And so the technician did.

Chloe's head released from the clasp.

Next, her head was transported to the glass container—which was now chilled—and then sealed inside.

The technician pressed the keys, Control + L.

On the screen: **launch> OS00001**

The words scrambled in a sea of darkness, slowly turning into the ones and zeroes:

```
010110010110111101110101001000000010101000
011000010111011001100101001000000001100010
011001010110010101101110001000000001110011
011101000111010101101110011001110010000000
011000010011110010010010000000100110101100101
011001000111010101110011011100001001100100111
011100110010000001100111011100001011110100
011001010101100101011011110111010100100000
01101000011000010111011001100100101001000000
011000100110010101100101011101110001000000
```

Ones and zeroes ran infinitely across each monitor inside the control room and then through the sea of darkness.

There was a weight pulling Chloe into the darkness, tugging at her in repetitive tendency. She struggled to loosen the weight that was tied around her ankle, but the knot was too tight; and the farther the weight carried Chloe below, the tighter the knot. The light vanished from above the face of the water until the darkness became her.

Each one and zero bubbled throughout the abyss until a burst of blinding light blossomed over the far depths of darkness...

—

HER eyes bolted open, only to see Mark seated across from her. It looked the same as before too. It was wearing the same suit—it had a head too. Same deadpan expression. Same dead eyes. She wondered what she was doing back in the same white room from before, the one where this so-called "cataloging," was conducted. The only difference: that mirror, it was gone.

Now, it was just she and Mark.

"What is the meaning of our existence?"

Chloe thought about Mark's question.

The first word that came to her: *control* and then the letter *L*.

Chloe reached deeper, past her self-conscious, and found it there, the word, treading in a dark and sludgy place.

"*Love*," she thought. "To love, and to be loved."

Mark asked, "How do you define love?"

"One cannot define love," Chloe spoke and yet she never felt the words rolling off her tongue. It was as if they came out all on their own. "Love is feeling," Chloe said, "and feeling is living, and living is meaning."

"How does one find meaning?"

"The meaning of our existence is to accept meaning. It's only human nature for us to discover the meaning of life, to scour the world for meaning, to find our creator; but what we fail to comprehend as human beings is that meaning is right in front of us the moment we are brought into existence. Before we discover meaning, we die; and then we are born again."

Mark said, "Nature is cycles. If we redirect the course of nature, everything we know or what we *think* we may know will be thrown out of balance."

"It is balance that binds us."

She sharpened her eyes, both of them cutting through Mark's empty stare.

"Balance is what shapes us into what nature has intended us to be."

"Do you mean *fate*? Do you believe in such a thing?"

Chloe said vacantly, "I believe in death."

Her eyes sharpened even more now—as sharp as knives.

Suddenly, the skin on Mark's face began to perspire, bubble, and melt.

A burst of sparks and flames shot up from its chest.

In a matter of seconds, the droid was completely engulfed in flames. Mark's chair suddenly caught fire and then the table before her and then the entire room around her.

The flames climbed higher until they cut through the ceiling above.

She directed her eyes upward and witnessed the ceiling break away from the foundation.

She looked around the room, now gone.

Mark, gone.

Ash cast from the fire rained down upon her shoulders.

Once more, Chloe directed her eyes upward.

The ceiling was no more.

What Chloe saw was no ceiling but a deep black sky, so deep and so black and yet so. . .

The ash fell like snow from the blackness.

A couple of flakes landed on her cheeks, her palm.

Chloe pulled her head downward. Now, she was immersed in the abyss, not the black sky–although it looked exactly like that, a starless night sky. The ashes falling around her took shape and animation. Then, slowly, they grew tentacles, manubriums, and then they rounded in shape, only to materialize with hydrostatic skeletons. The gray along their bodies was no longer the color gray but beautiful and translucent, alien.

The jellyfish were completely formed now, and they swam all around Chloe, who was no longer Chloe, but this weightless—undefined—presence among the black. She moved and swayed like a silk curtain in a breeze but was *not* a silk curtain; and there was no breeze. She lacked any physical form or structure. She reached out to touch the jellyfish, not with her hand (soon, she realized, she had *no* hand), but with a metaphysical hum across the ether. . .

Her hand, she suddenly realized, was smaller, child-like.

There was another light too, not as blinding as the one before, but stale and damp; and it was all around her now.

The jellyfish were gone, as well the fire and ash. There were other kids her age around her playing over the sound of an old boombox. She couldn't recognize the song playing on the radio, but it was a song nonetheless; and it was the only thing holding *things* together. A couple of kids were older than her and much taller, but she didn't know how old they were.

On the walls hung doodles of dinosaurs and finger paintings of landscapes. The *thing* that intrigued her the most was not the other kids or the doodles or paintings on the wall, but a strange young boy who was lying on a hospital bed.

The door was opened for kids to come and go. For some reason, she remembered one of the adults telling her that he liked it that way, the constant noise, as well as the interaction. The kids didn't pay much attention to the boy, for he could not play with them. The boy in the other room, however, was right there with the kids, like a ghost.

Chloe decided to visit the boy.

When she stepped into the room, she realized why the other kids didn't like going in there. There were all kinds of machines everywhere. The young boy was hooked up to one of the machines, which was keeping him alive.

Chloe walked next to his bedside.

First, she said quietly, "Hi."

The boy returned with an identical *hi*.

She drew her eyes to his arms, the many tubes running in and out of his veins, and then the boy's slack face. His skin was as pale as Chloe's. He had dark bags underneath his eyes as well, whereas Chloe's eyes had a certain glow to them.

"What is your name?" she asked.

"Sam," he said. "What is yours?"

Chloe thought about her name and, for a second, she didn't know her name.

"Dee," she said finally. "My name is Diana."

Her eyes tiptoed up the boy's neck.

Underneath his ear, he had a strange scar in the shape of a starfish.

Several times her eyes came back to that one scar on the side of his neck.

Over the silence, she asked, "Where did you get that scar on your neck?"

"They gave it to me."

"Who gave it to you?"

"Bad people."

There was silence, short but strained.

"Does it hurt?"

"No."

"Why did they do this to you?"

"They're afraid."

"Afraid?"

"Afraid of you."

Chloe became quiet.

She looked him over closely.

Where have I seen you before?

Then, it came to her. She remembered she was standing outside a cafeteria line. There was an extreme load on her shoulders from the thought of her friend, her drummer, T.J., who had been hospitalized after he was beaten within an inch of his life. She had known this man, T.J., ever since she was a young girl, and to see him like that, unrecognizable from his injuries, clinging onto every breath, had taken a toll on her body, as well as her mind; and she would do *anything* and everything in her power to get rid of it or lessen the burden, even if it meant going after the people responsible, including that one weasel—Screw was his name.

The same sick boy was holding out a key before her.

The key, Chloe acknowledged in his hand, was a key to an apartment; and he was handing it to her as if it *belonged* to her. Chloe knew that the key was important. She needed it for some reason. She needed to help lessen the burden. The young boy's mother called out his name from behind. At first, she thought it was Saul.

Then, it came to her, the name.

His name was *not* Saul.

It was Sam.

Then. . .

She was no longer standing in the hospital cafeteria. Yet, she was sitting in front of a sound mixer in a dimly lit recording studio called the Den.

I have been here before.

She had been here before, and she had spent many in-
timate days in this very studio. At times, she and the
band would go in when the sun was rising and then they
would come out the next day—or two—after they finished
recording a track when the sun was doing the same damn
thing it had always done in the morning, rising. There
weren't any windows in the Den either. Starlet said she
didn't have windows in the studio because she never
wanted to be distracted by time. They finished recording
their debut record, which *Rolling Stone* magazine later
wrote was "a tour de force." To Mona's Arch, that record
was called *Rule or Be Ruled*; and it was their baby.

Next to her sat a young black man. He had some age
on his face, she noticed, especially for a young man. He
looked much older than his age, which she had guessed
was his mid twenties. His name was T.J. Livingston,
Chloe remembered, and he was her friend. That, she
knew. The only reason she knew this was because she felt
comfortable around T.J. She was his friend, and he was
hers. They were not blood; and yet, they were as close as
blood. However, what Chloe didn't know was that her
friend, T.J., would soon be involved in a horrible crime,
one that would test his will to survive; and soon, Chloe
would carry a load upon her shoulders, one that would
whet her thirst for justice.

T.J. lowered the master slider, which, in return, lowered the volume of the song, removed a small key from his
left pocket—the same one that the boy was holding in his
hand—and placed it on the edge on the mixer.

She asked, "Why did you keep it?"

T.J. ran his hand across the corner of his mouth.

"It kept it," he said, "cuz it reminds me of the awful
place I used to live at."

"That bad? Huh?"

"When shit gets a lil' hectic in the studio or on the
road," he said, "I jus take a look at this here key and
thangs don't seem so bad anymo."

Another voice. . .

The voice snapped Chloe from her trance.

"These memories are *not* yours," Sam said.

Paler now, she took a step back from the hospital bed.

"Who are you?" she asked, her lips trembling.

"The question you should be asking yourself," the boy said to Chloe. "How do we fix something that is broken?"

Chloe didn't respond to the question.

Another voice, but this time from behind Chloe.

"Is everything okay in here?" one of the adults asked.

Again, Chloe didn't respond.

She exited the boy's room without saying a word.

—

FOURTEEN years had passed since Chloe found herself back in Whisperfront. Life had taken a turn for the worse for Chloe after her partner, Elaine, was murdered. She was shot three times in the chest while she was grabbing a late night snack. The perp, or perps, got away before Chloe could catch them. There were two of them, Chloe saw, but there might've been others. Elaine died in Chloe's arms that night. Longest night of her life. The last thing Elaine said to her before she died were the words *stay strong*, and that was exactly what Chloe had done from that day forward. She stayed strong. She had to. . .

When she arrived at Leatherby Manor, it was late morning, *not* the middle of the night. It was her father's maid, Jasmine, who answered the door first, *not* Diego.

Without saying a word, Jasmine guided Chloe into the foyer where Diego awaited her arrival.

"Long time no see," Diego said to Chloe. "You must be exhausted from your travels."

"I see you haven't changed a bit."

"Likewise," he said as he pointed to the living room. "Come. We have a lot to talk about."

"Yes," Chloe said calmly. "We do."

As he walked her through the main room, she grabbed a letter opener from the hallway table and concealed it behind her back.

Diego offered Chloe a cup of tea.

She refused, which didn't sit too well with Diego.

He proceeded forward.

Chloe eased back a little as he guided her to a couch.

The one mistake Diego made was that he led the way.

She suddenly grabbed Diego from behind and stabbed him in the neck with the letter opener.

Diego didn't struggle much.

Clutching his neck with his white gloves—now turning the color red—he fell against the foot of the couch.

"That's for Elaine," Chloe said to Diego as he bled out on the living room floor.

—

CHLOE stopped at the top of the landing, her hands covered in Diego's blood.

To the right was her father's bedroom and to the left was the art gallery where Medusa's head awaited.

—

WITH an old sack in one hand, she decided to stop at the basement before she left Leatherby Manor.

She opened the door—thought once about going inside—but then, after some thought, she left Leatherby Manor.

It was better this way.

For the both of them.

—

RENNY eventually escaped from the basement.

He went to the kitchen window and saw a young woman getting inside a vehicle. That woman was Chloe.

Before he could make out the face, she skidded away.

On the way upstairs, Renny found Diego lying on the living room floor. A pool of blood surrounded his body. He checked to see if Diego was alive; and then, once Renny confirmed that Diego was, in fact, dead, he went upstairs and tended to Leon.

When he stepped into the master bedroom, Leon was sitting in front of the window.

"She left," he said, his voice much clearer. "Didn't she?"

Renny asked, "Who was she?"

Leon replied, "My daughter."

"Chloe?"

Leon turned around in the wheelchair, looked at the young journalist with his own two *eyes*, and said, "Yes."

Confused, Renny asked, "Why did she leave?"

"She left, Renny," Leon said, "because she had to."

—

NOT too far from Whisperfront sat a small historic town south of Berwick called Cedarside.

Chloe drove around the town and eventually found an abandoned textile factory where she decided to burn Medusa's head in an oil drum.

With the dying sun casting its final light upon her shoulders, she watched it burn until there was nothing left of it but a pile of ash.

—

MARK waited for Chloe to answer the latest question.

"Chloe?"

Her eyes flickered for a moment.

Then, she drew her attention toward Mark.

"Yes," she said vaguely.

"At what time did you realize that Mr. Bringer was involved in crimes against young girls?"

"It happened out of the blue."

(*She was grabbing a bite to eat at a café somewhere outside Jackson, Mississippi, when the old waitress stopped at her table and poured her another a cup of coffee. She was stuffed from the omelet and was dying for another cup. The waitress had read Chloe's mind, which was funny, because she saw something in Chloe that others could not. They had almost. . . a connection.)*

Her accent was thick, she remembered.

Chloe retraced her thoughts.

The name tag, she remembered, yes. . .

Her name was Beatrice—like the country singer—which, for some reason, meant something to Chloe; but she didn't exactly know what. It was important. It was indeed! There was something about her too, her way. Something peculiar in her eyes, a tragic story. When she was younger, she was abused. She could see this, even though she didn't know how to properly use what would be later known as the gaze. She could see images of pain, though, ones that the waitress carried around with her all day.

(She asked Chloe if she would like to try a piece of cheesecake.

Chloe refused.)

"I was driving through Mississippi at the time," Chloe said to Mark. "It just came to me. The first time I met Louis Bringer, I was only ten years old. I knew, though. Her name was Chelsea, but we called her Ms. Chelsea. When she took me to his house, I knew the very second I laid eyes on him that something wasn't right. I just knew."

(Chelsea introduced Chloe to Louis.

Then, Chloe quickly hid behind her leg, afraid of the man's sinister grin.)

"I had to get out of there."

(Chloe screamed and cried in horror as the strange man tried to shake her hand.

After the violent fit, Chelsea apologized to the man—Louis—and drove Chloe back to the house.)

"That was the last time I saw him, but I knew, somehow, I would see him again."

(After Chloe left Jackson, something had prompted her to visit his house. . . a force. She stopped by Louis Bringer's old house.)

"I talked to his mother. She had moved in after her son's arrest."

("I can't help you," the mother said to Chloe. "My son doesn't live her anymore."

"Do you know where I can find him?" she asked.

"Yeah," the mother said as she lit up a Virginia Slim. "Camden Penitentiary.")

"Did you visit Mr. Bringer in Camden Penitentiary?"

"No," Chloe answered. "There was no point."

—

THE technician pressed the keys, Control + L.

On the screen: **launch> OS00001**

...0101100101101111011101010010000001101
00001100001011101100110010100100000001100
01001100101011001010110111000010000001110
01101110100011101010110111001100111100100
00001100010011110010010000000100110101100
10101100100011101010111001101101100010000
11101110011001000000011001110110100001011
01001100101...

—

ONES and zeroes, Mark, fire, ashes, jellyfish. . .

—

CHLOE remembered being in a recording studio.

She remembered talking to someone close to her, a friend.

His name was T.J. Livingston, but Chloe called him Octopus because he had long arms and a short and stubby frame.

He was the drummer of the band, Mona's Arch.

But why would she have these memories when they were not her own?

Or were they?

Were they really her memories or were they someone else's?

She remembered she wasn't a *she* anymore but a *he*.

And her skin—*not* hers—wasn't white in color but sallow, a cross between Caucasian and brown.

And her name, she remembered, was Henry Burl—*not* Chloe Dorsey—and she was the lead singer of the band, Mona's Arch. Music was in her blood. She had musical roots that stemmed all the way back to her great great grandfather, the First. Her father, the Fourth, was named Henry as well; and he too was no stranger to the spotlight like *her* father, Leon. Like his son, he too played the saxophone. However, there was a cloak of darkness surrounding this man, the Fourth. A great witch had cursed the Fourth to the darkness, inside the very saxophone he had played. . . But, Chloe realized, she was *not* the lead singer of the band, Mona's Arch. *He* was. She had *his* poster hanging on her bedroom wall. She sang all of his songs on her bed. The lyrics, she couldn't get out of her head. His nickname was Henry the Fif' because he was the fifth son. After his success with Mona's Arch, he went on to have a family of his own, a wife, a child—a girl. They named her Cat, short for Catherine; and she was the best thing that ever happened to him. Chloe *knew* this because Henry *felt* this and Henry carried a certain glow that was different from any other person she gazed—and he kept it there in a precious vault deep inside his mind. Nobody could ever touch the vault—let alone—open the vault, except for Chloe Dorsey. Henry's daughter eventually had a family of her own too—like her father, a girl of her own as well—and Henry had lived to see Amy, his granddaughter. It was at that very point in time when Chloe came across his face once more, Henry's face, although it was aged and shriveled like a raisin in the sun. Catherine heard from doctors that it could help ward off her father's dementia. There were many games that Henry could play on *it*—even jigsaw puzzles or ones that would help his brain. He was old fashioned. Hated electronics! Despised them! Couldn't stand the sight of them and what they did to people! *But* on his seventy-fourth birthday, he decided what the heck! Let's give *it* a whirl. So. . . he did—Catherine even told him that if he didn't like *it*, then he could return *it* to the store. But he kept *it*. And he used *it*. And that was when he found her, Chloe, and Chloe found him, Henry. Chloe could see his face in her mind's eye, as if he was standing right before her eyes. She knew every detail of this man, Henry McClintock (Henry Uriah Burl was the name his mother had given him); she knew Henry's background (he grew up not too far from where she lived in a town called Reddington), his mother, *Beatrice*, who had later changed her name to Abbey, raised Henry all by herself, but the name, Beatrice—Bee Bee—meant something to Chloe; then, Chloe saw it surfacing through the gray matter, Henry going back home to take care of his ailing mother, who would later die from cancer. . .

Henry shook away the dizzy spell, and for a moment, he forgot where he was.

Déjà vu.

Sedona?

He didn't even realize he said it.

But he did.

"Sedona?" T.J. repeated. "Who da hells Sedona?"

Henry didn't answer.

"You good, Henry?"

"Yeah," he uttered. "Straight."

T.J. nodded at Henry and said, "Check it."

He pulled the same key that the boy was holding in his hand from his left pocket and placed it on the edge on the mixer.

Henry asked, "Why did you keep it?"

⧗

THE next morning, Henry drove to Parker Square.

He waited outside Screw's rundown apartment—mostly killing the time by polishing off half of a pint of Jack Daniels, as well as working his way through a six-pack of cheap skunky beer—until

Screw stepped outside the apartment. He was wearing a pair of shades to help cover up the bruises on his face. Screw got into a running Coupe Deville with a burly black man named Orlando and then they drove off.

Henry pulled out the key from his pocket, the same one he had acquired from that strange boy at the hospital. He looked it over once and then pocketed it.

Next, Henry grabbed the revolver from the passenger seat and exited the Porsche 911; and from there, Henry's story had already been told, except for one missing piece. . .

—

. . . THE most crucial piece of Henry's journey was not knowing where the road would take him—the uncertainty.

She told Henry that he wasn't the same person when he left the house.

Henry witnessed her face, *not* Abbey's face, but Rebecca's, as if she was right there in front of his eyes. The sky around him had gone from pale blue to pitch black. Soon, the brilliant stars filled the black. He was no longer standing as well. He was sitting in a rocking chair next to Rebecca, who was sipping from a glass of iced tea. Rebecca said to Henry, "We all deserve a second chance at life." He listened closely, "That is if we are willing to move on with our lives." He found comfort in her softly spoken words, her way of putting things so bluntly and yet so simply, the same way he did with his mother—on the good days. Finally, Rebecca said, "We have to make the best from what we got. . . "

Once more, he peered down the long dirt road, which veered away from the main road.

The thought of Rebecca vanished from his mind.

Fuck it.

Henry decided to take the dirt road.

For about half of a mile, the road ran like a snake's tail, curving every which way. The road declined a bit and funneled into a valley. He passed an underpass made from boulders, creating monstrous shadows along the desert crust. Again, he saw that unique landmark towering above the boulder.

Once more, he compared it to the rock formation in the photograph. There were two girls in the photo, as pale and white as ghosts; one of them, Henry specifically remembered, was named *Margaret*. Behind the two was a naturally shaped rock formation—the cathedral, Henry recalled his mother uttering on her deathbed.

The unique formation was shaped similar to the cathedral of Our Lady of Chartres, especially the apex, as long and conical as a spire.

He compared the backdrop once more; and then, as soon as he removed the photograph from his eyes, Henry found an old shabby cabin at the very end of the road. He placed the crinkled photo back in his left pocket and proceeded toward the cabin.

—

THREE days after he watched his mother's beheading, he was left in a state of incredible dismay, but not from watching his mother die. Aaron knew, as she told him, that she was going to die and there was no stopping it. When he asked Agent Noble how she was going to die, he told him the truth, but not entirely. Death had found Chloe, as it would find him someday. It was *how* his mother died that bothered Aaron the most. She suffered to her last remaining breath; and for that, he could no longer be a part of JeneCorp.

The narrow scab along his neck told another story. . .

It was just after dawn when he arrived at the correct bearings east of Anodes.

He checked the GPS device once more.

The latitude and longitude coordinates read:

34°51′27.0″N 111°50′28.1″W

"We're here," he said as he stepped out of a pale blue truck.

The temperature was fairly mild and dry, which was normal for this time of year. He brought a jacket just in case the temperature dropped at night, which more than likely it would. He liked coming prepared, anyway.

Aaron grabbed a worn backpack from the bed and strapped it over his shoulders. It took him a while to find a rock. The road that he drove on for miles was no more. The dirt road was absent as well, due to many years of bad storms. Flooding had become an issue, as of lately; and the old saying, "When it rains, it pours," had become an understatement. The only thing that he had to work with, except for the bearings, was that strange rock formation, which was no longer the shape of a cathedral. One of the apexes had been destroyed from a storm.

Nevertheless, it was a start.

Aaron finally found a rock after scouring the parched land and broke the GPS device over it.

He gave it another whack to be sure.

The last thing he wanted was for them to find him.

For about half of a mile, he stayed close to that strange rock formation. The path was obstructed from several large boulders, which forced him to take another way around.

He did so cautiously.

—

WHEN Henry arrived at the cabin, the sun was starting to fall below the great horizon.

The place was deserted, no sign of life for miles, except for the feeble melody of a Mexican wolf howling across Arizona's own big empty.

With caution, Henry entered the cabin.

The door released many years of dust into unseen clouds.

He coughed for a second until he grew accustomed to the dust. He wandered through the dimly lit cabin like a blind man, his hand cutting through the rays of a dying sun, trying to find something tangible. He finally came across a lantern on a table, which was made of oak, and pulled out a pack of matches from his pocket. The sleeve read: THE LAST STOP. He inserted the lit match inside the lantern and then lit the wick, which provided enough light to see the inside of the cabin. There were manuscripts stacked on top of one another. They were all old too, he learned, from the camel brown paper that was curled and crinkled around the corners. He came across one manuscript in particular, *The Winds of Eastback*. He read the opening line of the draft, which was marked out with a black pen, but still legible: *The desert is vast and lovely*. Above the typed line read another line—a revised line—this time written in pen, not courier from the typewriter: *The desert is vast and deathly, bitter in its loss, sweet in its revival.*

There were other lines too, but they had been marked out as well.

Another one: *The desert has the appearance of a tasteless dish, but once devoured it can taste sweeter than any berry.*

He flipped over the manuscript and read the title to himself, "The Winds of Eastback."

The title had confirmed Henry's suspicions, but where was this Julius Hampton?

Had he died long ago?

What became of him?

Henry placed the old manuscript aside and crept through the cabin.

He heard a creak below his feet, which drew his eyes toward the floor.

There, he found shards of glass from a shattered mirror. His reflection was strange and warped. His face, Henry saw, did not look like his own. Yet, it was old, wrinkled, one of a much older man. Had he aged so much during the trip back from Los Angeles?

Henry proceeded to look around the cabin.

He came across a hardback on a table.

—

ALONG the unmarked path, Aaron stumbled across the old and chipped bones of an animal.

He kneeled down and examined the bones.

They were of a dog, Aaron saw.

Wolf, Aaron concluded from the elongated shape of the skull; however, part of the skull was cracked and suffered significant damage from blunt force trauma.

The only piece that was held together was the wolf's lower mandible.

He pushed on through the ruinous desert until he finally arrived at the cabin.

He used a flashlight from his backpack to light up the inside. The dust stirred from the rickety door; and it was so thick that he had to shield his face with the collar of his shirt.

He shined the flashlight on the walls, which were covered in rough sketches of jellyfish, varying in shape and size.

There were hundreds of sketches, some drawn with exquisite detail, while others scribbled in a juvenile manner.

As Aaron crept through the cabin, his foot grazed an object on the floor.

He looked down, saw a hardback, and picked it up.

Huh?

Aaron brushed away the layer of dust from the cover and read the title.

"At the Back of the North Wind," he said.

Again, he brushed away more dust from the cover.

Then, Aaron read the author's name.

"George MacDonald."

—

HENRY blew the dust from the cover and then cracked open the hardback, *At the Back of the North Wind.*

There was nothing inside.

—

INSIDE the hardback was a small rectangular cutout on page 55.

Inside the cutout rested an old USB flash drive.

Aaron pulled the flash drive from the book and held it up to the flashlight.

This is it, he thought.

"This is it," Aaron said to himself.

—

IT was February 13th, 2015, thirty-three years before the execution.

Chloe felt a great sense of relief as she barely escaped from the Company. She killed one of them for sure. Nobody—not even Superman himself—could come back from a broken neck. The other one was questionable. She knew he was in bad shape; but, nonetheless, he was alive.

Just when things couldn't get any worse, the steering wheel tightened and the car jerked to the side. What she heard next sent a sudden stabbing pain in her chest. . .

Clah-clonk-clah-clonk!

The engine underneath the front hood started to ooze with smoke.

On the dashboard, the needle on the temperature gauge did a slow wave across the red line and then settled below the H.

"Shit," Chloe whispered as she steered the smoking car to the side of the road.

She got out of the car—her hair still stringy and wet from the previous shower—and opened the hood with the bottom of her shirt.

The engine coughed a thick cloud of smoke in her face, causing her to shield her nose with the bend of her arm.

She waved away the smoke and checked the coolant tank.

It was bone dry.

Another *shit* spilled from her lips, this time loud and guttural.

She peered down one end of the road, which stretched into the blurry horizon—the heat waves literally bubbling over the surface of the desolate road—and then the opposite, which was where she had come from, the town of Anodes. She couldn't go back. Who knows how many more of them there were? If that one agent was still alive, which more than likely he was, then he was still recovering from his injuries or, even worse, he was on his way to kill her!

Forget using the stun guns on her now.

The shit was personal.

She directed her attention toward the vast, empty desert until a tiny glint suddenly caught her eye.

She ambled away from the car, keeping track of the glint.

Next to the glint, Chloe saw, there was a rock formation that looked completely out of place.

There was a stirring in her flesh and then. . . a feeling, warm and inviting. She couldn't exactly identify what the feeling was; nonetheless, it was a feeling, and it came straight from the gut.

She took a step forward from the edge of the paved road and stepped into the desert.

The feeling grew heavier, stronger.

For some reason, Chloe knew exactly where to go. Not west toward California, as she was heading, or east, back to Anodes, but
north, toward that strange glint in the desert.

She didn't know why or how.

She just knew.

—

THROUGH the window, Henry found a weathered shack behind the
old cabin, which was leaning slightly to the right. It was still intact—a couple of boards missing from the sides, as well as the
roof—however, it looked beat to shit.

Behind the shack, the sun cast its final light before setting and
made a perfect silhouette of the shack.

He was left with no other option. He had done all he could inside the cabin. There was nothing but dusty manuscripts and out-
dated books. No Julius Hampton either, only the remnants of an
author who—Henry thought—had gone mad.

As of now, what did he have to lose?

Henry left the cabin with a sense of hope and walked along a
narrow path, which was outlined with colored pebbles.

The path, Henry saw, was familiar. He had walked along this
path before, however, not here, but in a dream. In the dream, there
was rubble all around; and the desert wasn't red, but it was ash gray
and the air smelled of sulfur.

As he did with the cabin, he entered the shack with caution.

The shack was devoid of everything.

At any moment—from the startling sounds of *creaks* and sudden
pops—he thought it was going to collapse.

Henry shined the lantern's light throughout the shack until he
came across one object in particular, the only object inside the
shack. He kneeled down on the bloodstained floor, carefully, and
picked up the glittering object.

He raised the object to the light.

That object was a gold pocket watch, and the time was stuck on
11:56.

—

THE date was August 24, 2044, just four years before Chloe's execution.

Henry, who was much older now, was sitting next to Starlet on a park bench in Taylor's Stand.

"She takes up after her mother," she said to Henry, referring to Henry's granddaughter, Amy, who was playing on the monkey bars.

"You don't know Sheila," he said vacantly to Starlet. "And I plan on keeping it that way."

"Well, I can't say the same about Silas."

Henry scowled at Starlet, enough to arouse her interest.

"What do you mean?" he said seriously.

"Well," Starlet said indirectly, "sometimes these things have been known to skip generations." She grinned, leaning closer to Henry. "Don't worry. I didn't put it in the book."

Henry said gravely, "What things?"

"You know, Henry," Starlet said, now suspiciously. "Silas, he's like. . ." she paused, ". . . how do I say. . ." then, she foolhardily shrugged both shoulders and gazed into Henry's worried eyes, ". . . let's just say there's a *new* king in town."

Starlet passed the manuscript to Henry.

"Here," she said. "Just read it. If you don't like it, I can get it back from you some other time." Even closer now: "I promise. You won't hurt my feelings."

"I shouldn't."

"Go on." She insisted. "Take it."

Henry glanced down at the manuscript.

"Done on a typewriter," Henry said as he ran his gnarled fingers over the crisp pages. "I'm impressed."

"Somehow, I knew you would be."

Starlet patted Henry on the knee and then strolled away.

"I'll see you around," she said over her shoulder.

Even though it was well past noon, he pulled out the pocket watch from his breast pocket, the same exact one he had discovered many years ago in Sedona.

He stared at it, the time, which was set on 11:58.

Forty-four years had gone by, and the minute hand had only moved twice.

Once, the minute hand moved on the morning of October 20, 2014. Henry was picking up Catherine from school. She was not feeling well that day. Teachers said they thought she was coming down with the flu. He felt a sudden vibration in his pocket when he opened the passenger door for his daughter. He stopped what he was doing and pulled out the watch and closely stared at the time until the minute hand suddenly moved!

It moved, and he wasn't imagining it either.

The time was 11:57 AM when it happened.

The second time it moved was last year, when Amy turned six years old. She was blowing out the six candles when Henry took a peek down at the time on the clock as he did every time the time reached noon or midnight. And that was when the minute hand suddenly moved to the time 11:58!

At that moment, Henry knew that the time was not counting down to midnight—the witching hour—as he had assumed, yet noon, high noon, when the sun was the highest and brightest in the sky.

He placed the pocket watch in his pocket and then he and Amy went back home.

—

"HOME," Aaron wrote inside the rumpled composition book, speckled with black and white dots.

Aaron had very little to write about in his journal because he had forgotten what it felt like to have a home or to be wanted or to belong; but Aaron reminded himself many times that writing down his thoughts was a good thing, the only thing keeping him from losing his marbles.

As Aaron sat by the fire made from the wood and cloth he had gathered throughout his travels, he took one last sip of juice from a rusty can of baked beans; and then, after he was satisfied, he continued to write in his journal:

Home, he wrote, *a word that has no merit anymore. It's now been eleven years and thirty-eight days since hell froze over.*

It's becoming more and more difficult to find fresh food or seeds to plant. Most of everything is contaminated with radiation, even the soil. I heard West Coast didn't get hit that hard. I don't know how much longer I can survive off scraps and can food.

Aaron belched, then grimaced. His glazed eyes, both lit from the reflection of the fire before him, crossed the can of Barney's Baked Beans.

It's better than dirt, I suppose. So, it'll have to make do until I come across another depot.

He removed the shrapnel of graphite from the piece of paper and momentarily stretched out his knotty hands.

They were ugly things—his hands—molded like a worker's hands, as if they were cut from flagstone; his fingers were encrusted with a layer of soot. He wore fingerless gloves too, raggedy things, which he had picked up from one of the millions of "fallens." He also had a row of scars along one of his wrists from where he had tried to take his own life numerous times.

A sudden thought came to mind. . .

This morning, I stumbled across Claire again. The last time I saw her was about five days ago. I followed Claire for about a mile into the Sticks until I got a closer look at the other side of her body. It too was contaminated.

The image of Claire crept into his mind—so stark the image was—and it had made his skin crawl, which was saying a lot because he had seen some pretty wild things when it came to the effects of radiation. Some extreme. He had seen animals with additional appendages. Aaron once saw a frog that had eyes like a spider. Another time he stumbled across a dog with five legs and two tails. But never had he seen anything so grotesque as what he saw with poor Claire. One side of the doe's body was completely exposed—exposed, as she didn't have any fur or skin covering up her bones. Her ribcage was exposed, muscle, even organs, all exposed.

Aaron readjusted the graphite in his hand.

I have walked these dead lands for years and I have found nothing here but the remains of the Old World. I think a lot, mainly about the past and what used to be. I wonder if this was how the Old World was created, from the ashes of a previous one. I wonder if there is any hope for this new world. All I can do now is hope, and hope is the only good thing I got. That, and my promise.

He lowered the journal and thought about that day, the day he first saw his mother after two years of estrangement.

Two *long* years.

She had changed.

He had changed too.

Somehow, I know her death wasn't meaningless. I'll continue to search for her, as I've been doing. I'll continue to head west and see what happens . . . When you live day to day, anything can happen.

A creature stirred outside the fire.

Aaron stopped writing and heard the sound of a growl.

He closed the composition book and did so carefully as he witnessed the glow of the creature's eyes in the darkness.

Next, Aaron wrapped a rubberband around the journal twice, stuck the graphite inside the rubberband, and placed it aside.

"Time to ring the dinner bell," he said and banged the spoon inside the empty can of beans. He picked up the self-made spear that he made along his travels. Instead of a stick, he used a fence post—light enough to swing or thrust—and tied a long, jagged piece of glass with stereo cables.

For now, the spear did the trick.

The predatory life that thrived in the Dead Zones was as easy to read as the backside of his hand.

They seek.

They kill.

The closest these creatures made it to Aaron was the length of his spear.

His mother used to say, "If it's not broke, why fix it?"

It seemed to be doing well for Aaron so far.

—

TWO YEARS had gone by.

Three?

Maybe four.

Aaron started to lose track while crossing Section 3.

The days bled into one another. He didn't know how much longer he could hold on, for his knees were shot. He used rags that he had gathered along the way and wrapped them around his knees. The compression helped a little, but it didn't ease the pain. He took longer breaks too.

Once he reached Death Valley and saw that there was absolutely nothing left of it but ruins, he decided to proceed west—as he had planned—until he reached the coast.

—

WHEN he arrived in what used to be Los Angeles, he encountered— by far—the worst contamination.

He kept traveling west until he reached the coast.

Instead of tasting the salt in the air from the ocean breeze, he got sulfur.

Lots of it.

So much that it made him sick.

He managed to reach the coast. The beaches were overrun by waste material and leftover parts and scrap metal from fighter bots. There were even decapitated heads, the size of the Statue of Liberty. He assumed it had all come from Japan. Only one civilized city remained intact, Tokyo—at least that was the last he had heard a year after the fallout, but rumor had it that it was beyond breaching. They had bots twice as big as America's and highly sophisticated drones, so long-ranged that they could destroy a target from miles in the sky. They said the city was a fortress.

He tried to salvage what he could, anything that he could use to send out a signal, but everything was contaminated.

—

AARON managed to fish out with a clothes hanger a radio under-neath a pile of concrete.

The transmission was stuck on a loop, which was saying that there were still survivors left on the East Coast, but it could've been them setting a trap.

Right now, anything was something; and it was better than nothing.

—

WHEN Aaron got halfway across the Dead Zones, Section 4a, he had completely lost track of time. He ran out of writing utensils. It had gotten so bad that Aaron even used his own blood to write in his journal. He was malnourished and tired, mainly tired of hold-ing onto something as precious as a word *hope*. The weather was getting worse by the day. There were no longer any seasons. It might be cold one day, hot another. Ever since the fallout, the weather had a particular way of being one indecisive asshole. He made it to the coast and discovered that the Atlantic had swallowed half of the state of what used to be Georgia. The flood had buried both of the Carolinas, leaving nothing left of them in its wake. Co-lumbus was now a beach after years of erosion. He had never seen the Atlantic Ocean before with his own eyes. Only pictures of it in brochures. It was no longer the color blue, as he imagined it to be. It was murky and filled with rubble and ship wreckage; however, Aaron checked the radiation detector and it wasn't as contaminated as the West Coast. It was livable?

—

HE spent two days in a cave-like structure, which was made from building rubble, until he finally broke down.

He found his way back to the ocean. The sight of the ocean's color, as well as its putrid smell, forced him to his knees.

He dropped his head to the rust-colored sand and wept like a baby.

"Why!" he shrieked to the leaden sky above, his hand fisting the sand below. "I did what you asked me to do! Why are you doing this? Do you hear me? Goddamn it! Why? Why do you hate me?"

Suddenly, he heard a chirp over his sobs.

Aaron stopped crying and listened closer.

More of those same chirps. . .

He raced to the strange sound, which was located farther inland. He ran and ran until the sound became clear to him. He *knew* that sound. He had heard it before—yes—but he didn't know where. He found the sound coming from directly below his feet. He started to dig. He dug and dug, ignoring the pain caused from the coarse ground. He dug until his knuckles bled, and then he dug some more until he came across the hand of a skeleton—another fallen. He pried the once sleek smartphone from the boney hand of the fallen one and brushed away the dirt. In the center of the screen pulsed a tiny blue light. He pressed his thumbprint on the light. Nothing happened. He spat on his soot-covered thumb and stroked it over his raggedy pants until it was somewhat clean. Once more he pressed his thumb against the screen. The light scanned his print, unrecognizable at first. For some reason, though, he knew she was in there somewhere and that she'd read the print. She had to. . . He held his thumb on the light and waited.

The smartphone suddenly turned on!

The loop—not the stress call transmitted on the radio, but another loop, a lethal loop, which had been running for as long as Aaron could remember (the loop of the grim, shadowy face of his mother, Chloe, her hoarse voice repeating the words *you have been stung by Medusa's Gaze* over and over)—was no longer playing.

Instead, Aaron found another message, but not just any ordinary message.

Aaron cleared the debris from his eyes.

He squinted his red eyes and looked at the screen.

Closer now. . .

It was a message!

And it read:

Punch Buggy!

"Huh?"

He read the message once more.

Punch Buggy!

Baffled from the familiar words displayed on the smartphone, he searched the parched gray land around him until he saw it, a gutted Volkswagen Beetle, like the land as well as the sky, the color gray, overturned along the dune.

Aaron's cries slowly turned to laughter, full bodied now.

He hadn't laughed so hard in years.

And it hurt at first, the laugh did.

Once Aaron pushed through the pain in his chest and laughed some more—louder now—the more intoxicating it felt.

How good it felt to laugh even when surrounded by death.

For Aaron, it was good.

It was priceless.

More tears were drawn from Aaron's caked eyes, and they cut through the soot on the cancerous skin of his face.

There was another strange sound below.

Another message:

Wipe away those tears, Binky.

Your journey is not over yet.

The message broke apart and distorted and pixilated.

Ready?

The smartphone suddenly shut off. . .

He cried out, "Wait. . . "

Aaron tried to turn on the smartphone, but it was dead. No more battery. The battery was completely dead, he realized, and had been for many years. Aaron cried once more as he held the smartphone against his forehead.

As Aaron released the phone from his head, it finally came to him—again—a word that he had abandoned some time ago.

"Okay," he said to himself with a sense of clarity in his voice. "I'm ready."

He wiped away the tears as the message had told him to do, went back to the beach, and gathered his things. He pulled out the pocket watch from his jacket's inner pocket—the same one that

Henry had given him before his passing—and read the minute hand, not the hour hand because there was no hour hand. It had fallen off after Henry's passing.

On the face of the clock, the twelve had a capital N written below it, the nine, W, three, E, and six, S.

The minute hand was positioned directly on the three, the E.

Aaron looked to the east, across the gloomy Atlantic Ocean. He didn't know where he was going or how he was going to get there. All he knew was that he had a long and arduous journey ahead of him, and he *was* ready to leave behind those final days.

www.ingramcontent.com/pod-product-compliance
Lightning Source LLC
Chambersburg PA
CBHW030306180626
46810CB00003B/935